Gerber opened the
Stars and Stripes

As he looked at an inside page, he felt his stomach turn over. Smiling out at him was a picture of Sean Cavanaugh, looking as if he had just escaped from high school. Gerber stared at the youthful face, short hair and the white shirt and dark tie. He thought of the young man who had evaded the draft by volunteering for active duty in the Army and found himself in Vietnam before anyone in the World knew where in hell it was.

Below the photo of Cavanaugh was another of two people. The captain had thought of Cavanaugh's parents as elderly, but this couple didn't look old. They looked miserable. The woman was holding a handkerchief to her face as the man, his face contorted in anguish, accepted the Congressional Medal of Honor from the President.

A scrap of powder-blue cloth, Gerber thought, sprinkled with white stars, and an iron wreath with a star in the center and the word Valor engraved on it.

Certainly not worth a son.

VIETNAM: GROUND ZERO
SOLDIER'S MEDAL

A GOLD EAGLE BOOK FROM
WORLDWIDE

TORONTO • NEW YORK • LONDON • PARIS
AMSTERDAM • STOCKHOLM • HAMBURG
ATHENS • MILAN • TOKYO • SYDNEY

First edition April 1987

ISBN 0-373-62705-X

Printed in Canada

AUTHOR'S NOTE

The report of the NVA attack on Special Forces Camp A-102, March 9-10, 1966, is based on official U.S. Army and U.S. Air Force records and after-action reports. Major Bernard F. Fisher, USAF, was awarded the Congressional Medal of Honor for his heroism at Camp A-102 on March 10, 1966.

New U.S. Special Forces Camp A-555
(Triple Nickel)

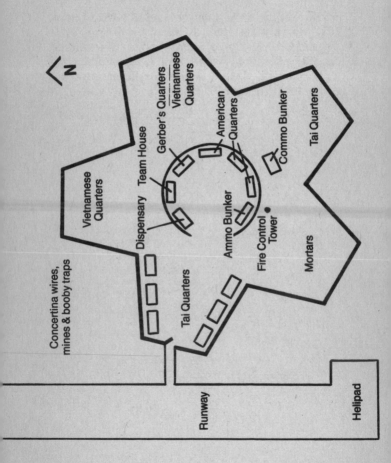

VIETNAM: GROUND ZERO
SOLDIER'S MEDAL

PROLOGUE

U.S. ARMY SPECIAL
FORCES CAMP A-555
NEAR THE CAMBODIAN
BORDER IN THE THREE
CORPS TACTICAL
OPERATIONAL AREA,
RVN 1966

Army Special Forces Sergeant Sean Cavanaugh fell against the rear of his foxhole in Listening Post One and stared at all the fucking dead men lying in the short elephant grass and in the rice paddies near him. From the direction of the camp three hundred meters away, he could hear the rattle of small arms fire, the crash of mortars and the bang of grenades. Above the camp he could see the flares hanging beneath their parachutes as they drifted toward the ground, a line of smoke describing their path through the sky. With his right hand he grabbed the heavy PRC-10 to request support from the camp's mortars, but the radio had been so shot full of holes that it was useless, and the field phone had disappeared in a grenade blast that had wounded Sergeant Luong and killed Corporal Lim.

The last of their ammo had been used during the attack when the fighting had degenerated into a hand-to-hand conflict, and Cavanaugh and his tiny command of armed strikers had been forced to use their worthless rifles as clubs.

Now Luong was struggling to pull the equipment away from a dead VC. Grunting with the effort, the wounded sergeant tried to free the pouch that contained extra magazines for the AK-47 that he had already taken. He dropped the used clip from the weapon and slammed a new one home as the enemy reappeared in the flickering light of the distant flares and ran toward him across the open ground.

When Cavanaugh saw them coming, he picked up his carbine, but it was empty, and he had no spare ammo for it. Clawing at his holster, he drew his .45 and fired rapidly one-handed, the weapon jumping with the recoil.

It was as if the enemy had suddenly sprung from the ground. At first there was no sound, but then a noise began, a low growl that built slowly until it was a roar. The VC began shooting, firing their weapons as they ran, trying to cut down the defenders of the listening post.

As one of the enemy reached the edge of the foxhole, Cavanaugh fired a last time, his pistol only inches from the VC's stomach. The man dropped as if he had been poleaxed, but another materialized right behind him, leaping across the body and colliding with Cavanaugh. They fell together, rolling over in the confined space of the hole. Cavanaugh kicked with his right leg, twisted his body and found himself facing the enemy. He swung with the empty pistol and felt it connect, shattering the bones of the VC's face. Cavanaugh scrambled closer, grabbed the man around the neck and squeezed as he hit the enemy again with the pistol. He heard a sharp crack as the skull caved in, and the man slumped lifeless to the ground.

To his left he saw Sergeant Luong struggling with a VC. The enemy kicked out, knocked Luong to the ground and drove his spike bayonet through the young Vietnamese's side. Luong suddenly sat up and grabbed his attacker around the throat, pulling him forward, squeezing as he hit him in the face with his fist. The two fell back to the ground.

Cavanaugh tossed away the useless pistol and picked up his carbine, swinging it like a baseball bat. He knocked one man off his feet and smacked a second in the head with such force that the wooden stock splintered. As a third man leaped at him, Cavanaugh dropped the rifle and grabbed his entrenching tool, chopping with it as if he was clearing vines from a jungle trail.

Unaware that a growl was bubbling in his throat, that all the RFs with him were dead and that the VC were trying to escape, he kept swinging the tool. He smashed the blade into the side of a VC, knocking him to the ground. Then, screaming, he hammered the fallen enemy. The sergeant leaped to his right, balanced on the balls of his feet, his knees flexed, his head swiveling right and left, looking for more of the enemy. But they were suddenly gone, as if the ground that had given them birth had swallowed them again.

For a moment Cavanaugh stood there, his eyes shifting from one body to the next, watching them, waiting for them, as a light mist seemed to drift out of nowhere, hiding some of the dead. Cavanaugh fell back against the side of the foxhole, his breath rasping in his throat, the sweat trickling down his face to stain the collar of his torn and dirty fatigues. He listened, but the night was suddenly quiet as even the sounds of the firing from the camp died away.

Then out of the darkness he heard a moan, a single low cry of pain. When he looked up, he saw one of the enemy soldiers standing there, a gaping wound in the side of his head glistening wet and red in the moonlight and the flares. The man seemed stunned but stumbled toward Cavanaugh, who felt fear knot his stomach.

Around him more of the enemy were coming to life. Men missing hands or feet or legs. Men with uniforms ripped by bayonets and knives, with wounds in their stomachs and chests and entrails hanging from their bellies. Men who had been dead moments before now with new life breathed into them, coming at Cavanaugh, who stood helpless, holding the entrenching tool in one hand and the broken carbine in the other.

"No," he shouted. "You're dead." He tried to take a step back, but there was nowhere for him to go. Under his breath he mumbled, "No, not again."

Suddenly he was awake, sitting on his bunk, his back pressing against the wall of his hootch. His OD T-shirt was soaked with sweat. Cavanaugh could feel it crawling down his back and dripping from under his arms. He lifted a trembling hand to his neck and rubbed the back of it, surprised at how wet it was. His mind flashed to the walking dead men, the corpses from the battlefield that haunted his sleep, and suddenly he had to stand up, to move somewhere, as if the very act of moving would take his mind off the horrors that were there.

He stopped in front of his metal locker, opened the top drawer and felt under his clean uniforms for the bottle he had stashed there. Army regulations prohibited enlisted men from having alcoholic beverages in their quarters, but Captain Gerber winked at such things. The Special Forces rarely followed all the Army's regulations.

Cavanaugh pulled the cap from the whiskey bottle and drank deeply, feeling the liquor course down his throat and pool in his stomach, spreading liquid fire. He exhaled through his mouth and took a second deeper drink. This time he rocked back on his heels and looked at the hootch's rafters, at the screen there and the light filtering through it. To his right the gentle rise and fall of the chest of the form on the cot told him that Sully Smith, another of the team's NCOs was still asleep. Cavanaugh grinned to himself. Since Sully was asleep, it meant that Cavanaugh hadn't cried out as he sometimes did. He took a third pull and felt his hands steady and the sweat begin to evaporate.

Glancing again at the sleeping Smith, Cavanaugh capped the bottle and tucked it away. The sergeant stood and moved back to his cot, then sat down. He rubbed a hand through his close-cropped hair and sighed. He was getting better. Now the dream only came two or three times a week. Immediately after the battle to defend the listening post, he had had the dream every night, sometimes twice a night, and it had been so frightening that he had tried to stay awake twenty-four hours a day. Now with the booze it was something that could be controlled. He didn't lie awake for hours shaking but only until he could get to the bottle. He wasn't sure whether the booze stopped the anxiety or if it was the act of getting it. Drinking water or tomato juice or smoking a cigarette might have done it. Anything that took a little time and gave him an immediate goal. Something to do.

Cavanaugh lay back with his hands under his head and stared up at the silk from a parachute flare that was draped over the rafters of the hootch. Dirty white silk that hid the tin of the roof and was a standard interior decorating item in South Vietnam. Hanging through the middle of it was a ceiling fan that spun slowly, stirring the fabric and the air.

Cavanaugh concentrated on remembering everything he could about flying saucers, a subject that had interested him since he was a kid. He could barely wait for morning, for the opportunity to get up and out and do something else. He didn't want to tour the defenses or check on the status of the strikers in the bunkers and on guard because the captain would notice that and wonder why he was out every other night doing it. It wasn't normal, and Cavanaugh knew that the last thing he wanted was to appear abnormal.

1

SPECIAL FORCES CAMP
A-555 NEAR THE
CAMBODIAN BORDER

After a long hot night spent sweating under the mosquito netting of an Army cot and listening to the quiet squeak of the ceiling fan as it slowly spun, Sergeant Sean Cavanaugh was ready for the patrol to begin. One hour before sunup he had gotten out of bed and searched through the metal wall locker where he stored his uniforms, gear, civilian clothes and, against Army regulations, his space ammo. He had done it by touch, feeling the coarse fabric of his jungle fatigues, the rough hardness of the web gear and the cool smoothness of his M-14.

Like a man with arthritis, he moved slowly, trying to dress noiselessly and wondering if he should wear the thick OD socks the Army issued. During long patrols the socks tended to slip and rub against the foot and ankle, causing blisters. He sat on his bed, staring at the dark shape of his naked foot outlined against the light plywood floor, and thought about it. Finally he tossed the socks back into the locker and pulled on his newly issued jungle boots with their green nylon panel along the ankle.

When he finished dressing, he grabbed his web gear, pistol belt and spare canteens from his locker, shouldered his weapon and carefully latched the metal doors. As he stepped toward the entrance of the hootch, he glanced back at Sully Smith, who slept on, a dark, almost invisible shape concealed by the wispy green mosquito netting. Cavanaugh flipped him a salute and walked out into the muggy heat of the Vietnamese morning.

The sergeant stepped down into the red dust of the compound and hesitated. When he had first returned to the camp, he had told Fetterman that it looked completely different. Then he learned that it *was* different. Almost the entire camp had been burned to the ground and then rebuilt. Next to his hootch were two more like it. They were frame structures, the bottom half covered with unpainted, overlapping one-by-sixes that looked like clapboards; the top half of each hootch was screened with wire mesh to allow any breezes to pass through. The roofs were covered with shiny corrugated tin that was supposed to reflect the sun's heat. But the tin rusted quickly in the wet Vietnamese environment so that the roofs took on a golden glow in the daylight.

Across the compound were more hootches for the officers and the team sergeant. The team house, a long building used as a mess hall, rec room and briefing room, also squatted there. Next to it was the commo bunker, obvious because of the antennae sprouting from it like the whiskers of a cat, then the dispensary, a heavy sandbagged structure, one of the ammo bunkers, a weapons locker and the supply room. All this was crammed into the redoubt, an earthen breastwork that was five feet high and topped with barbed wire. Outside was the rest of the camp: the mortar pits, the hootches for the strikers and their families, the fire control tower and a line of bunkers that surrounded the camp, giving it a star-shaped look from the air. The runway and main helipad were outside the six strands of concertina wire, rows of claymores and booby traps. There was a secondary emergency-use helipad that was inside the compound but outside the redoubt.

Cavanaugh settled his boonie hat on his head, slipped into his web gear—the giant Randall combat knife was taped upside down to the left shoulder strap—and headed for the team house. The knife was a replacement for the one he had lost during the defense of the listening post, paid for by the members of the team as a "welcome home" present. They had mail-ordered it from Ironmonger Jim of Anoka, Minnesota. Cavanaugh had accepted it quietly and then spent the better part of two days sharpening it until it could slice easily through the toughest material or the softest flesh. He had blackened the blade so that it wouldn't flash in the sunlight or glint in the moonlight.

He entered the team house and saw Captain MacKenzie K. Gerber sitting at one of the six square tables that were already set for breakfast. The tables occupied the front two-thirds of the hootch. A bar separated the back third from the area where the tables were. Behind the bar was a stove, an oven and a storage area for canned foods. A single Vietnamese woman worked back there, preparing the morning milk by mixing cool water with powdered milk. To the left of the entrance as one came in were the remains of the old refrigerator—the plug had melted in the fire when the old team house burned—and a new refrigerator that seemed to have taken on the personality of the old one. It rarely worked and, when it did, froze everything solid.

Gerber was reading an overseas edition of *Time*, turning the pages as if the whole issue disgusted him. He glanced up at Cavanaugh and greeted him. "Morning, Sean. You're up early."

"Yes, sir," Cavanaugh replied, slipping into a chair near Gerber. "Got a patrol this morning."

Gerber flipped the magazine closed and set one hand on the back cover. "It's still early. And you don't have to bring all your equipment with you."

"I know, sir, but Sully was asleep and I didn't want to wake him." Cavanaugh unbuckled his pistol belt and grinned sheepishly. "Besides, this is my first patrol since I returned, and I guess I'm a little nervous about it."

"No reason to be nervous, you've done it all before." Gerber got up and moved to the coffeepot for another cup.

Cavanaugh stood and slipped out of his gear, piling it on the floor next to his chair. He walked to the bar, grabbed one of the individual boxes of Kellogg's Corn Flakes and a pitcher of milk, the sides of which were beaded with sweat. Ice cubes in the pitcher clinked against the metallic sides as Cavanaugh returned to the table.

As he sat down, Sergeant First Class Justin Tyme, the light weapons specialist, entered. Tyme was a tall, slender, sandy-haired young man who was normally quiet and seemed to be overly serious at times. Unlike Cavanaugh, he wasn't wearing his full field pack. He was dressed in jungle fatigues that were clean but not starched, and he hadn't bothered to tie the laces of his boots. He nodded at Gerber, who had returned to his chair, then waved at Cavanaugh. Tyme collapsed into the chair nearest the door, rubbed his face with both hands and said, "I'm not ready for this. Let's take the patrol out about noon, or better yet, about five."

Cavanaugh set his cereal and milk on the table and sat down. He pushed the perforations on the front of the small box, spread open the flaps and dumped the contents into his bowl. He splashed milk on the cereal, sprinkled it with lumpy sugar and began to eat.

Tyme watched Cavanaugh, then glanced at Gerber. "Any orange juice this morning, Captain?"

"I think we have some Tang."

"Christ, that's not orange juice, that's colored water."

"Then no," said Gerber, "we don't have any orange juice. We have some lousy coffee and some powdered milk and about half a case of warm beer."

Tyme rubbed his eyes with his hand and then, without looking, gestured at Gerber. "I'll take one of the beers."

"Before the patrol?" asked Gerber.

"Yes, sir. Unless you object?"

"No, Boom-Boom," said Gerber, "I don't object to a single beer, although I'm not convinced it's the best eye-opener."

"It's better than Tang."

Gerber got one of the beers out of the refrigerator and set it in front of Tyme. "I'll give you that." He turned his attention to Cavanaugh, who was hunched over his bowl. "I'll see you two at the gate before you leave."

As Gerber left the team house, taking his coffee with him, Tyme picked up his beer and moved to the table where Cavanaugh sat. He took a deep drink and made a face at it. "I wish we could get some real orange juice in here."

"Yeah," said Cavanaugh, "it's a little early in the day for beer."

"Sometimes that's all there is to drink. Powdered milk and powdered orange juice and powdered eggs—none of it tastes real. And shit, in Saigon they're probably dining on real eggs and real steaks and telling the press that war is hell."

Cavanaugh dropped his spoon into his bowl and pushed them away. "I'll meet you at the gate," he said, making it sound more like a question than a statement.

"Sure." Tyme nodded. "Make the equipment check. Make sure they all have the ammo they're supposed to carry. Sometimes on these routine patrols they leave the ammo back. Don't like humping it through the jungle."

"I know my job," snapped Cavanaugh.

"I'm sure you do," said Tyme. "It's just that you haven't been out here for a while."

Slowly Cavanaugh got back into his gear. He adjusted the shoulder straps until they rested comfortably on his shoulders, buckled his pistol belt and walked to the door. For a moment he stared out, looking into the deep blue of the sky overhead. Back to the west was a line of black clouds that suggested afternoon storms. As he left the building, he said over his shoulder, "Meet you at the gate."

Since the camp had been destroyed during the fight to recapture it and since it had been redesigned afterward, the gate was now on the west side about a hundred meters from the runway. Two large bunkers that housed heavy machine guns, two .30-caliber machine guns and 90 mm recoilless rifles guarded the flimsy gate and graded road that led to the Triple Nickel. Immediately inside the gate was a low wall of green rubberized sandbags that could be used as an additional machine-gun nest if the enemy was getting too close.

Most of the Vietnamese strikers stood near the low wall, their packs on the ground at their feet, their rifles stacked nearby. A couple of them sat staring at the ground or talking to one another. Cavanaugh approached them slowly, cautiously, wondering if any of them remembered him or if they blamed him for the deaths of the RF strikers during the defense of the listening post. He could see nothing in their eyes that suggested they knew what had happened, or maybe it was just something in their past and they assigned no blame for it.

He leaned his rifle against the sandbags and said, "Let's get this show on the road."

The Vietnamese responded slowly, getting to their feet and helping each other seat the packs on their backs. They all picked up their weapons, a collection of rifles from the Second World War and Korea with a few of the new M-16s thrown in, and formed a ragged line facing away from the sun.

Cavanaugh wiped a hand over his face, which was sweat damp in the early morning heat. He moved down the line, checking the packs, looking for the food rations of cooked rice and fish heads. He had to make sure that each man was carrying his allotment of spare ammo, that each had his share of the squad equipment—spare ammo for the M-60 machine gun, extra rounds for the M-79 grenade launchers and extra batteries for the radio.

Moments later Tyme approached from the redoubt. He walked up to Cavanaugh and put a hand on his shoulder. "We about ready to bug out?"

"They're all set," Cavanaugh told him. "Want me to check your pack?"

"Take a look if you want," said Tyme, "but shit, Sean, we're only going to be out twenty-four hours. I can carry everything I need for that in my pockets."

"Just a thought."

Tyme turned to watch Gerber as he came toward them. No one saluted because saluting only identified the officers for the enemy.

When he was close, Gerber asked, "You ready?"

"Yes, sir. Everything's set."

Gerber glanced upward, noticing that there were only a few wispy clouds directly above him, ignoring the black ones to the west. "Let's watch the pace," Gerber warned them, "it's going to be hot and miserable out there."

Tyme wiped his face and then rubbed his hand across the front of his fatigues, leaving a ragged stain. "Yes, sir, it sure is. Anything else?"

"Not that I can think of." He moved closer to Cavanaugh. "Sean, you've been out of this for quite a while. Don't be afraid to say something to Justin if you're not used to humping in the bush."

"No problem, Captain," said Cavanaugh. "I spent some of my time in Saigon working out. I can handle it."

"Okay," said Gerber. "Have fun, then. I'll see you when you get back. Good hunting to the both of you."

Tyme nodded to one of the Vietnamese. "Hanh, take the point. Move on out for about two hundred meters and halt."

Hanh shrugged and trotted through the gate and down the rough red dirt road that led to the runway. He crossed it and stepped onto the new shoots of elephant grass growing up through the thin layer of ash.

Gerber stood watching as the rest of the twenty-man patrol exited the camp and crossed the runway, heading to the west. He put a hand to his eyes to shade them and then turned at a noise beside him.

"They get off?" asked Master Sergeant Anthony Fetterman, the team's operations sergeant. He was a small man, both short and skinny, and looked as if a stiff breeze would blow him over, yet he had a strength that surprised and amazed the rest of the men on the team. He had a dark complexion and claimed to be part Indian, sometimes Aztec, sometimes Sioux and sometimes Cherokee.

"Yeah, they got off," responded Gerber. "Just left. Be out of sight in the trees in ten, fifteen minutes."

"Cavanaugh went out?" asked Fetterman.

"Yeah," said Gerber. "Cavanaugh went out."

"Good. We need to have a talk about him, and I figure'd it would be easier with him off the camp for a while."

TYME WATCHED THE POINT MAN cross the runway that had been sprayed with peta-prime, and then followed with the patrol. They entered into an area where the grass had burned off, the tiny green shoots pushing up through the black ash and red dust. The strikers kicked up tiny clouds of ash and dust that seemed to hang in the air with no breeze to stir them.

The column moved across the open ground, trying to reach the trees before the sun climbed high and baked them with its merciless heat. Tyme could see their path behind them, a wavering line of red in the nearly unbroken field of black and gray and green.

Up ahead a finger of jungle reached toward them. At first it was little more than a few bushes and a couple of trees, but it widened rapidly into a deep green belt of coconuts, palms, teak and mahogany that stretched skyward. The broad leaves of the trees were interwoven in a canopy that shaded the ground and stopped the rain. If they could reach it before the sun got too high in the sky, it would make travel a little less difficult. It would still be hot and humid, almost like hiking through a steam room, but the sun wouldn't sap their strength like an energy vampire.

Tyme was already sweating when they entered the jungle. He could feel it on his back and under his arms. The go-to-hell rag around his neck absorbed some of the sweat, but not enough to make him comfortable. Tyme wiped his forehead with the sleeve of his jungle jacket and wished that it would snow. Just once and for only an hour or so. The constant hot weather was getting to him. Vietnam was a land of seasons. Two of them. Hot and dry, and hot and wet. He wasn't sure which season he was in, however, because it had rained heavily the day before.

In the jungle the patrol slowed, walking carefully, each man watching the ground around him for signs of booby traps or ambushes. They had found a game trail that looked as if it hadn't been used by anything for a while. The growth wasn't nearly as thick as it was in the surrounding jungle, and Hanh was able to make his way through it without using his machete. The strikers and the Americans stepped over fallen palms, pushed branches out of the way, tried to avoid the brambles of the wait-a-minute vines. Slipping through the jungle, the idea was to leave no clue that they had been there, but to look at the ground, searching for hints that Charlie might be near. Charlie was as good as they were, however, sometimes better at concealing his movements.

Tyme glanced up then, and through the breaks in the vegetation, he could see the strikers leaping from the trail, taking up firing positions, facing right and left so that they were guarding each other's backs. They crouched among the bushes and grasses, their rifles held ready, watching the jungle for hostile movement as they had been trained to do. Cautiously, Tyme made his way to the head of the patrol where he found Cavanaugh lying on his stomach, his rifle out in front of him, his chin nearly on the ground as he stared straight ahead.

Tyme approached him, knelt and said, "What you got?"

Cavanaugh turned his head slightly so that he could look back over his shoulder. He grinned at Tyme. "Trip wire. Step back a couple of meters, and I'll see what it does."

Tyme backed off and watched as Cavanaugh reached out with his M-14. Then he pulled it backward until the wire was against the weapon's forward sight. He jerked it once and dropped the rifle to the ground.

There was a popping of vegetation as if something large was crashing through the jungle. An instant later there was a whoosh as a small tree that had been bent back was suddenly freed; it swept across the trail and smacked into the trunk of a large palm. Tyme could see that a dozen sharpened bamboo stakes had been driven into the palm by the force of the impact. They were about knee-high and designed to take out one or two strikers on patrol, maiming but not killing them. The philosophy behind the booby trap was that a wounded man required two other patrol members to carry him to safety, but a dead man was just dead.

Tyme stood and looked at the trap again. Ingenious in design and use of local flora. He wasn't sure that he liked the way Cavanaugh had triggered it, although no one had been hurt by it.

Cavanaugh climbed to his feet and brushed the dirt and dead vegetation from the front of his fatigues. "That takes care of that. Ready to move out?"

"Let's give the men a break," said Tyme. "We've been at it for better than an hour."

"Fine with me." Cavanaugh stepped off the trail and into the jungle, almost disappearing into the vegetation. He crouched and took a drink from his canteen, then poured some of the water on his go-to-hell rag. Draping it over his head, he let the evaporation of the water cool him.

Cavanaugh dropped his pack, rummaged through it until he found the pound cake from one of the C-ration meals that he carried. He opened the tin with his P-38, got the cake out and ate it quickly. He took another drink from his canteen, draining it, and then sat back to look at the tiny patches of sunlight that managed to find their way through the thick foliage. On the branch of a small bush, he saw a spider spinning a complex web that seemed to fill one patch of sunlight.

When Tyme passed the word for them to saddle up, Cavanaugh slipped on his pack, adjusted the shoulder straps until it rode high on his back and then smashed the spider's web with his boot, crushing the insect before he stepped onto the trail.

Moving into thicker jungle, they were forced to follow the trail more closely because of the tangled vegetation. Vines clogged the undergrowth like a net strung between the trees. The canopy, now three layers thick, kept the sun from penetrating to the jungle floor. They were wrapped in a continuous twilight with deep black shadows that shifted in the light breeze. Instead of cooling them, it only reminded them of the muggy heat. Far overhead they could hear the rumble of thunder and knew that it was raining. They could smell it, the fresh, clean odor brought by the breeze, and they could hear it falling into the trees above them, although the water didn't reach the ground yet.

As they continued to move, the rainwater trickled down the trunks of the tall hardwood trees and fanned out onto the broad leaves of the bushes before dripping onto the soft earth of the jungle floor. The men nudged the bushes forward, then let the branches slap back, hitting the others behind, covering each with the moisture that was now seeping into the jungle. They looked as if they had been standing in an open field in the storm. Even though they could now tell that the rain above them had slowed, they knew that the water would continue to seep through the vegetation for hours.

The patrol halted again, and Cavanaugh moved forward slowly, using the undergrowth and trees for cover until he found Tyme crouching at the edge of a clearing. There, uprooted trees, broken bushes and a thick growth of elephant grass had taken root on the sides of a gigantic bomb crater. Before he could say a word to Tyme, he noticed a slight movement in the vegetation on the other side of the crater. A single VC, dressed in black pajamas but wearing Khaki web gear and carrying an old bolt-action rifle, was moving through the clearing slowly, watching the ground near his feet.

"Do we take him?" Cavanaugh whispered.

"Not yet," answered Tyme. "Let's see if there's anyone behind him."

Cavanaugh slipped off the safety of his weapon and aimed at the enemy, tracking him as he progressed across the clearing.

"Don't shoot him," warned Tyme.

"I'm not planning on it," Cavanaugh replied. "I'm just keeping him covered." His weapon didn't waver from the VC.

The man walked into the trees and then reappeared, his shoulders hunched against the light rain. He moved to the edge of the crater and looked down into it, as if he had found something fascinating in the bottom of it. He reached back toward his hip and then seemed to look right at Cavanaugh and Tyme.

Cavanaugh didn't hesitate. He pulled the trigger of his weapon twice and watched as the enemy soldier was slammed backward violently, one hand flung in the air, the other clutching his rifle in a death grip. The man disappeared into

the grass, rose slightly as if to look at his killers and then fell
back out of sight.

"What in the hell did you do that for?" snarled Tyme.

"He saw us. He was going for a grenade."

"Christ, Sean, we could have captured him. You didn't have
to shoot him."

"I thought he was going for a grenade."

"Okay." Tyme pointed to three of the strikers behind them
and indicated positions for them. Then, moving slowly, Tyme
got to his feet and entered the clearing. He skirted the edge of
the crater, looked at the clear water that filled the bottom and
then approached the dead soldier. He stepped on the hand that
still was clutching the rifle and bent over to jerk it free. With
his foot he rolled the body over, saw the two bullet holes in the
chest—neat, circular holes in the man's black pajamas, the
edges glistening bright red. Near his hip the VC carried two
hand grenades and a canteen. Tyme looked at the grenades,
the canteen and the water in the bottom of the crater. Cavanaugh could have been right. Or the man might have been about
to refill his canteen.

Tyme shrugged, pulled the web gear from the body, checked
for documents and insignia that would give Kepler and his intelligence boys something to work with.

"I think we might as well head back to the camp," said
Tyme when he reentered the trees.

"Let's see if this guy had any friends," said Cavanaugh.
"We might be able to get a couple more."

"I doubt it. If he had any friends, they would have scattered by now. Searching the jungle won't do us any good. Besides, I've seen all I was supposed to. Sean, why don't you take
the point."

"You're the boss," Cavanaugh said, but he didn't ask for a
direction of march. Instead, he began to backtrack, following
the same path that they had used to get to the clearing.

GERBER AND FETTERMAN were going to have their talk in the team house after they had finished their checks of the camp's defenses to make sure nothing had happened to them during the night, but Sully Smith was there eating his lunch. Gerber stopped in the doorway and turned to look at Fetterman. "Let's go over to my hootch."

They crossed the compound and entered the small structure. It was similar to the two- and three-man hootches used by the others, only smaller. Gerber had his Army cot shoved against one wall under the off-center ceiling fan. Next to the bed was an old ammo crate, which had been turned on end to serve as a nightstand. Near the door was a small Army field desk that could be folded into a cube about two feet on each side. When opened and assembled, however, it was a moderate-sized desk painted a sickening green. A metal folding chair sat behind it while two more occupied the space in front of it. The furnishings weren't quite as nice as the ones Gerber had had before the camp was burned.

"Take a seat, Tony," he said. He pulled a bottle of Beam's out of the desk's bottom drawer. "You want a touch?"

"Not now, Captain. It's a little early."

Gerber smiled and put the bottle away. "Don't let it be said that I wasn't the gracious host. Now then, what do you have on your mind?"

Fetterman crossed his legs and ran his thumb and index finger along the crease in his jungle fatigues. He studied his uniform intensely for a moment and then asked, "Are you aware that Cavanaugh has been having nightmares?"

"I think that's to be expected," said Gerber, "given the circumstances."

"Yes, sir. But they've continued. I've seen all the classic signs. He's the last one to leave the team house, usually the first one up, looks tired, and I've seen him out inspecting the bunker line at night when it's someone else's turn to do it."

"I know that," said Gerber, nodding. "Saigon advised me of it, but they also pronounced him fit for duty. They should know what they're doing. Besides, he asked to come back here."

Fetterman smiled. "I don't know why you would think that Saigon knows what it's doing. I know I don't trust those doctors. Hell, Captain, they're a bunch of college boys who've never been out in the real world. What are they, twenty-six, twenty-seven years old and given commissions as captains and majors because they've spent eight, nine, ten years in college? They blow into Vietnam and pretend they understand the stress of combat based on the Saturday afternoon matinee."

"I would think they're qualified to practice medicine," said Gerber.

"I do, too, sir. But they don't understand the nature of combat. How could they? They've never been in it. They see it in the movies and think of it as something adventurous. People die, but they die cleanly. Little, neat holes in a shirt with a little fake blood splashed around, and in the next feature the guy is up and around again. They know about the clichés, but they don't know the business. They've never seen a man killed in battle, his uniform soaked in blood, with the top of his head missing, or an arm, or all his guts stacked on his chest."

"There a point to this, Tony?"

"All I'm saying, sir, is that you've got a bunch of doctors in Saigon who don't understand that we have to work closely with the men here, get to know them, and who don't understand that Sean should be home chasing cheerleaders, not defending a listening post to the last round of ammunition and the last of the men under him. They think they know about the trauma of combat, so they pronounce him fit for duty."

Gerber nodded and reopened the desk drawer to get the bottle. He opened it and took a drink, feeling the liquor burn its way down his throat, before handing it to Fetterman. "You building up to something, Tony?"

"Just that I think we should watch Sean carefully. You didn't see him when I found him. Just sitting there holding that broken carbine and blood-covered entrenching tool, the bodies of the strikers lying next to him and the LP surrounded by sixty, seventy dead VC. Real dead men. Not the Hollywood variety. Real blood soaking and staining the grass and the buzz of the flies. That's what's always missing in the movies, the sound of the flies."

Gerber stretched his hand out to Fetterman, who still had the bottle. The captain took a last drink before corking it. "No, I didn't see him there, but I did see him in the hospital. I did talk to the college boy doctors, and although they may not understand combat, they do understand the nature of the human mind. They told me that Cavanaugh feels guilty because he survived and all the men around him died. He feels he should have died with them, that he let them down by not doing so."

Fetterman started to speak, but Gerber held up a hand to stop him. "Yes, that's pretty standard, and you don't have to go to school for ten years to know that, but what you don't know is that the Army contributed to that feeling. You, Bromhead, me, everyone here thought that we should get Sean the Medal of Honor. That was one piece of impressive fighting, but there were no other survivors. We couldn't prove that Sean had been brave. You know it and I know it, but we couldn't prove it. The Army isn't going to accept our speculation that Cavanaugh set up the defense because if he hadn't, they would all be dead, including him, and there would have been no enemy bodies around his position when we found it."

For a moment Gerber stopped talking and looked out the door at the bright afternoon sunlight and the red dirt of the compound and part of the redoubt. "So we couldn't get him the Medal of Honor no matter how much he deserves it," he continued. "The regulations worked against us. Then we had Crinshaw sitting in his office in Saigon not wanting to do us any favors, so he made sure that anything we put Cavanaugh in for was downgraded, and so on. By the time the award was approved, it was just a regular medal, nothing great, and Cavanaugh took that to mean that the Army disapproved of his actions."

"But that's just—" Fetterman began.

"Ridiculous," Gerber finished for him. "Of course, but Sean, being as young as he is, doesn't understand the politics that go on in the Army. Crinshaw doesn't want us to look good because he believes that makes him look bad. He isn't concerned with the emotional state of a nineteen-year-old kid. So Cavanaugh sees the reduction of his award from what should have been the Medal of Honor as proof that he's no good. Shit, Tony, we should have put him in for it, anyway, even if there was no way he could get it."

"Yes, sir," agreed Fetterman. "It looks good in the record, even if the award isn't made."

"So what you don't know is that the Army doctors asked me to let him come back out here, nightmares and all. It wouldn't look good in his record if I had turned him down because of what had happened."

Fetterman got to his feet. "I understand that. But it wouldn't look good if he's marked down as KIA. Especially if you have to mark Boom-Boom KIA, too."

Gerber didn't move. He stared at Fetterman for a moment. "I'm aware of that. But I'm aware that we owe Sean a debt, as well. We'll just have to watch him closely until we're satisfied that the problems have been resolved."

"Yes, sir."

2

OUTSIDE THE MAIN
GATE OF CAMP A-555

Sergeant Sean Cavanaugh halted the patrol shortly before dusk about four hundred meters from the main gate. Using the PRC-10, he alerted Bocker, who had the radio watch, that they would be coming in and would pop smoke, selecting yellow because the bright color would be easier to see in the fading daylight than one of the darker colors. As soon as it was acknowledged, Cavanaugh waved the patrol forward. They crossed the airstrip again, trying to avoid stepping in the pools of peta-prime, and entered the camp. When the gate was closed, Cavanaugh turned to face the Vietnamese strikers and called, "Weapons and equipment check in thirty minutes. Then we'll break for chow."

Tyme watched as the men headed toward their hootches to clean their weapons, even though Cavanaugh was the only man to have fired his rifle. From the direction of the redoubt, he saw Captain Gerber and Sergeant Fetterman coming toward them.

When they were close, Gerber asked, "How'd it go?"

"Pretty routine, Captain. One enemy KIA. We've got the weapon and gear but nothing for Kepler." Tyme stopped talking and looked at Cavanaugh who was standing there, too, listening.

"Who gets credit for the KIA?" asked Fetterman.

"Cavanaugh," Tyme said quickly.

"Good job, Sean," said Gerber. Then he turned to Tyme. "Justin, I'll want a full report in my hootch as soon as you can get there." He looked at Cavanaugh. "Sean, please make sure that the Viets get their weapons cleaned."

"Yes, sir." Cavanaugh took off after the Vietnamese.

"Now," Gerber said to Tyme, "how'd it really go?"

"Just fine, Captain. It went just fine, only. . ." He stopped talking, looking at the retreating back of Cavanaugh, the darkening of the camp as the sun vanished and then at Fetterman.

"Only?" prompted Gerber.

"A couple of little things bother me. Nothing I can really put my finger on."

"All right," said Gerber, nodding. "Let's adjourn to my hootch." But before he moved, he said, "Either of you care for a beer?"

"Is it cold?" asked Tyme.

"Surely you jest," said Gerber. "Of course it's not cold. Cool maybe, if we're lucky."

"Then by all means," said Tyme, "I would love to have a beer."

As both Fetterman and Tyme headed for Gerber's hootch, the captain stopped in the team house long enough to grab three cans of Oly from the refrigerator, which had broken down again. Then he trotted across the compound to join the two men in his hootch. Fetterman sat in the chair behind the field desk, and Tyme took one of the metal chairs on the opposite side. Gerber handed a beer to Tyme and then set one on the desk for Fetterman.

"I'll get out of your chair, Captain," said Fetterman, rising.

"Don't bother," responded Gerber. "I'll just park on the bunk here." He opened his beer with the church key from the nightstand, then tossed the opener to Tyme. The weapons specialist caught it, opened his can, then slid the opener across the desk toward Fetterman.

"Now," said Gerber, "what's bothering you about the patrol? Cavanaugh fuck it up?"

"No, sir, he didn't." Tyme took a swig of his beer and sat still for a moment as if formulating his answer. "Little things are bothering me. A couple of little things."

"Such as?" asked Gerber.

Tyme looked at the floor and told them about the trip wire. "He just yanked on it without examining it. If it had been tied to a grenade or an artillery round, it could have killed four or five of us."

"But it was a mechanical booby trap, right?" said Gerber. "Maybe he did know. Maybe he had seen something that had clued him about the nature of it. Did you ask him about it?"

"No, sir, I didn't. Not standing there in the jungle."

"Okay," said Gerber. He shot a glance at Fetterman, who was sitting with his eyes closed, listening and drinking his beer. Gerber prompted Tyme. "But that's not the only thing."

"No, sir, it's not. I'm simply not convinced we had to shoot that VC. Sean said that he thought the guy had spotted us and was reaching for a grenade."

"But you don't believe that?"

"I believe that Sean believes it, but I don't see how the guy could have seen us, hidden in the jungle the way we were. The light wasn't right for him to have seen us. Besides, he was standing there calmly. I think he was reaching for his canteen. I think he was going to fill it from the water in the bomb crater."

"So he fired and you didn't," said Gerber. "You think he was wrong to shoot?"

"That's the problem, sir. He may have been right. The VC may have been reaching for the grenades. Maybe he'd planned to grab one and toss it before hitting the dirt. Perhaps Sean was right to fire, although he shot a little faster than I would have."

Gerber nodded and took a long pull at the beer. "Anything else?"

"He took the same path back to the camp. I was wondering a little about him, so I told him to take the point, but I didn't give him a compass heading. He began backtracking on our trail."

Now Fetterman opened his eyes. "You ask him about that?"

"Sure, Tony. He said that we're supposed to be out there looking for the VC. He said that since we'd seen no signs of them, other than the one guy out for a stroll, this way we might be able to draw them out."

Gerber rubbed his chin. "That's a tactic I'm not sure I approve of, but it is pretty standard. I can't really fault his thinking on it."

"No, sir," said Tyme, "but you see what I'm getting at. It's a lot of little things."

"But none of them really mean anything," said Fetterman. "You said you didn't ask him about the booby trap. Maybe he'd seen something that you hadn't and knew what it was going to do. You said the guy might have been reaching for his grenades, and backtracking on a trail is fairly routine practice when trying to draw out the enemy."

"All true, Tony," said Tyme. "All true. I don't know what it is, though. There's something about each of those incidents that doesn't sit right."

"Sergeant—" Gerber put the meeting on a more formal level by the use of Tyme's rank "—is there something more to your concern than your feelings? Did he mistreat the men? Show a lack of concentration? Make any kind of blatant, stupid mistake?"

"No, sir. He moved well in the jungle. He didn't seem overly jumpy or nervous."

"Would you object to going out on patrol with him again?"

Tyme hesitated before he answered. "Ah . . . no, sir."

"You don't seem very sure of that."

"I wouldn't object to going out with Sean, sir." He grinned. "As long as it's not tomorrow."

"I can understand that." Gerber got to his feet. "Why don't you get yourself some hot chow and prepare a written report on the patrol. Leave out your personal observations of Cavanaugh's behavior. Keep it limited to the facts."

As Tyme was leaving, Gerber said, "Tony, I'd like to talk to you for a moment."

"Yes, sir. I had a feeling you would."

"Well, sit down and tell me your thoughts on all of this."

Fetterman dropped into the metal chair that Tyme had vacated. He continued to sip his beer while Gerber reached over to turn on the electric light. There was a single bulb suspended from a rafter in the center of the hootch.

"I think Boom-Boom has reinforced what we talked about earlier," said Fetterman.

"But once again we're stuck with nothing that you or anyone else could point to. A series of incidents that have very natural explanations."

"It seems that we've got a situation here," said Fetterman.

"A very delicate situation, Master Sergeant," said Gerber. "A very delicate one."

"I could set up a little test if you like," Fetterman suggested. "Maybe force something in an environment where it won't matter. That is, here in the camp rather than in the field where a bunch of people could die."

"All right, Tony, I'll leave this in your hands. You let me know how it turns out."

Fetterman stood. "I can have an answer for you in about an hour."

"Don't rush it," said Gerber.

"It's no problem, Captain. It's a simple test."

As soon as he had finished inspecting the strikers' rifles, Cavanaugh headed to his hootch. On entering he saw that Sully Smith was gone and decided that a drink was in order. He leaned his weapon against the wall near his locker, dropped his pack to the floor and then knelt so that he could reach into the top drawer. As he pushed his clothing aside, he noticed that his hands were shaking. Cavanaugh held his right hand out in front of him and watched it tremble.

He grabbed his bottle and sat back so that he was leaning against the side of the cot. For a moment he sat there, puzzling over the vibrations in his stomach, the queasy feelings that rocked him. He tried to figure it out but couldn't. There he was in camp, relatively safe, and still he was shaking, the sweat covering his forehead and sliding down his back and sides. It wasn't that hot out, and the perspiration felt clammy and cold.

Cavanaugh pulled the cork from the bottle, sniffed the opening and grimaced at the strong odor. Placing the bottle to his lips, he drank swiftly, not tasting the bourbon. He felt it in his belly, spreading a warmth through him that seemed to overwhelm and smother the feelings of anxiety.

As the liquor calmed him, Cavanaugh leaned his head against his cot and closed his eyes, breathing out through his mouth. He waited for a few moments, then took another long pull, this time holding the bourbon in his mouth before swallowing it. He concentrated on the liquor, letting it take over, forcing all the other thoughts from his mind.

The sound of boots on the floor surprised Cavanaugh, and he looked up to see Fetterman standing in the doorway, holding something in his hand that was wrapped in a poncho liner. Cavanaugh had no idea how long he had sat on the floor. The light from the sun had disappeared and had been replaced by the dim glow of the camp's electric lights.

Fetterman's eyes shifted to the bottle that Cavanaugh held loosely. For an instant Cavanaugh thought about hiding it, but the damage had been done. Besides, Fetterman had no idea how much had been in the bottle or how much he had had to drink. To cover his momentary embarrassment, Cavanaugh held up the bourbon bottle. "Care for a snort?"

"No, thanks. The captain just gave me a beer." He reached over and turned on the lights.

Cavanaugh got to his feet slowly, brushed off the seat of his jungle fatigues and then sat on his cot. He picked up the bottle, corked it and set it on the floor near his feet. "What can I do for you?"

Fetterman stood in the doorway and studied the man in front of him. He was still wearing sweat-stained fatigues. His hair hung limply, and his boots were muddy. It looked as if he had come straight from the Vietnamese quarters. The master sergeant's gaze was drawn to a small frame nailed to the plywood at the head of the cot. Inside the frame was the medal that Cavanaugh had won for defending the listening post—a medal that clerks got for doing their jobs well, that officers got for showing up at the office for six months, that was given out during transfers and retirements and that nearly everyone in the Army had received at one time or another for doing almost nothing other than being in the Army. It did not suggest that Cavanaugh's defense of the listening post had been heroic or extraordinary. It suggested that his resistance had been something routine.

Fetterman sat on Smith's bunk. "How're things going for you?"

"What do you mean?"

"You getting settled in okay? Everything as you expected it to be? Any problems that you didn't anticipate?"

Cavanaugh took a deep breath and sighed. "No, nothing. It's just like I expected it to be. Camp's changed quite a bit, but I expected that after I heard it had burned down."

"How do you like the climate? Must be quite a change from hanging around those air-conditioned rooms in Saigon."

"Well, I find it a little hard to sleep at night. I'm not sure how you guys do it. Seems like the minute I hit the sack, I'm covered with sweat and the air stops circulating. I'm trying to get used to the heat and humidity again, but it's going to take time."

"Yeah," Fetterman agreed. "That can be a problem." He stood, moved to the door and stopped. "Oh, I almost forgot. I've got a little present here. A little something I think you'll appreciate having back."

Cavanaugh got to his feet and took a step forward. "What is it?"

Fetterman slowly unwrapped it and held it up. "It's your entrenching tool. The one you had at the listening post. I cleaned and oiled it for you to keep it from rusting. It was badly messed up when I got my hands on it. Watch the edge, it's real sharp. But I guess you know that." Fetterman kept his attention focused on Cavanaugh's eyes.

But there was nothing unusual there. Almost no reaction at all, except maybe some disappointment. Disappointment that the present hadn't been something more substantial, like the replacement combat knife had been. Cavanaugh reached out, took the handle of the E-tool and held it up as if it was a baseball bat. Then he grinned.

"Feels the same, Master Sergeant. Thanks for hanging on to it. I didn't think I would ever see it again." He set it on the floor next to his rifle and picked up the bottle of bourbon. "You want a snort?"

Fetterman reached out. "Yeah. I think I will take one." He grabbed the bottle, drank deeply and handed it back. "Listen, Sean, if there's anything you need, you let me know. We'll work it out."

"Thanks, Sarge. I appreciate it."

"Yeah, I'll catch you later." Fetterman stepped out into the compound and found Gerber sitting on the sandbagged wall outside the team house, drinking a beer while he waited for the ops sergeant.

"How'd it go?" he asked.

Fetterman shrugged. "Test was a flop. No reaction at all. Just took the damned thing and set it on the floor before offering me another drink."

"You think he might have a problem in that area? Drinking too much?"

"I haven't seen anything like that. Hell, Captain, we all suck down the booze pretty good. You've got a beer there, and you've started that ritual where we pass the bottle of Beam's around, taking a healthy belt."

"The difference, Master Sergeant, is that we're not using the booze to drown our emotions. We don't use it to sleep or to wake up."

"Yes, sir." He was silent for a moment. "Cavanaugh took that damned E-tool, looked at it and set it down just like he had ice water in his veins."

"All right," Gerber said. "Maybe we're overreacting here. Maybe we don't have a thing to worry about."

"I don't know, Captain. It's not his veins that I'm worried about."

3

INSIDE SPECIAL FORCES
CAMP A-555

VC were everywhere. Thousands of them swarmed out of the trees a hundred meters away, rushing across the open rice paddies and fields of elephant grass. They were screaming and whistling, urged forward by bugles, shooting from the hip.

Sergeant Sean Cavanaugh jammed a new magazine into his M-1 carbine, locked the weapon against his shoulder and began pulling the trigger rapidly. He could see the rounds strike the enemy. Blood appeared on their chests, spurting from the bullet holes, and dust flew up as stray rounds struck the ground.

But the enemy wouldn't die. They wouldn't fall. Cavanaugh knew that they were hit. He could see it. He could see the impact of the rounds. But the enemy just wouldn't die.

Glancing to the right, he watched Luong fall, his arm severed at the elbow and a neat round hole right between his eyes. Lim disappeared in the explosion of a grenade. Cavanaugh was suddenly alone, the RF strikers dead at his feet. Stuck with a weapon that wouldn't kill.

And then he was awake.

Sweat covered him, dripping from his face as he sat bolt upright in bed. He rubbed a hand over his head, wiped his palm on the OD T-shirt he wore and took a deep breath. If they would only fall when he shot them, the dream wouldn't be so frightening. It wouldn't make him feel so powerless, so impotent. If only he could stop some of them... But he couldn't. They kept coming, thousands of them, springing to life, all of them running directly toward his listening post while the men with him died horrible, vivid deaths.

He swung his legs out of bed and put his bare feet on the dirty floor. A chill enveloped him, and he shivered, even though he knew the outside temperature had to be in the eighties. He stood and took a single step toward his wall locker.

From far outside he heard a quiet, muffled pop. Looking at the door, he counted silently, waiting, and a moment later heard the explosion. By its sound he could tell that it was exploding gunpowder that signaled a mortar landing and not the flat loud bang of the 122 mm rockets that Charlie sometimes launched at the camp.

Cavanaugh didn't move right away but knelt by the door, looking out into the moonlit compound, waiting for a second round. He didn't see it land but heard it impact farther away than the first, which meant that the mortar rounds were moving away from him. He got to his feet and waited, watching as some of the men—he recognized Gerber and the new executive officer, Lieutenant Greg Novak—sprinted from their hootches and through the opening in the redoubt, probably heading for the fire control tower.

There was a moment of silence as if the war and the world had stopped, and then the rounds started falling faster than before. Cavanaugh dived to the ground and rolled to his right, stopping next to the sandbags of his hootch. He wondered if it would be safer inside or out. The VC were aiming at the buildings, but they rarely hit anything. The safest place was the commo bunker because it was completely sandbagged and

could take a hit from a rocket. Mortars just tore up the sandbags.

There was a brilliant flash as a round detonated outside the
redoubt, and Cavanaugh heard the shrapnel raining down on
the tin roofs of the hootches. Two more explosions came in
swift succession, one at the center of the gate and another at
the dispensary, which erupted in a ball of fire.

The moment there was a pause in the firing, Cavanaugh
leaped to his feet and started running toward the burning
building. He found one of the strikers sitting on the ground,
his hands pressed to his ears and blood streaming down the
side of his face. Cavanaugh knelt, took the man's head in his
hands and turned it so that he could examine the wound in the
moonlight. It seemed to be a superficial cut above the hair-
line, but it was bleeding heavily. The man looked dazed, as if
he had bumped his head. Cavanaugh grabbed the striker under his arms from behind and dragged him between the team
house and Gerber's hootch.

Satisfied that the wounded man would be protected by the
sandbags around those structures, Cavanaugh ran back out
and saw that the dispensary fire was spreading. There was an
explosion on top of the redoubt, and Cavanaugh dived for
cover as it seemed that the world around him was blowing up.
Over the ringing in his ears, he heard the whoosh of a rocket
engine and then the loud, devastating bang from a rocket detonating close to him. Moments later shrapnel and debris
rained down, hitting the ground around him and bouncing off
the tin roofs of the hootches. All around him was the odor of
cordite, the acrid stench of the gunpowder from the missile's
warhead. He glanced to his right and saw that the team house
was burning, part of its roof missing. He ran to the door and
looked in. One man was lying on the floor, his legs tangled with
an overturned chair. Cavanaugh rushed in, threw the chair
aside and lifted the soldier to his feet. As he helped the dazed
man from the burning building, he noticed that it was Derek

Kepler, the team's intelligence specialist. At the door Cavanaugh heard someone moan.

He set Kepler on the ground outside, then looked around, but it seemed that everyone had taken cover. Suddenly aware of the heat from the fire, he turned and ran back into the team house. Cavanaugh stopped at the door and held up a hand to protect his face. Another body. He leaped forward and grabbed the man's shoulders, dragging him away from the flames. This time it was Sam Anderson, one of the camp's demolitions experts. As he pulled on Anderson's shoulders, he saw someone on the floor partially hidden by an overturned table and obscured by the dense smoke.

Cavanaugh pushed Anderson out the door, letting him fall clear of the team house. The young sergeant rushed toward the table as part of the bar collapsed, sending up a shower of sparks. He pushed the table aside and reached down for the last man. It was Sully Smith. Cavanaugh grabbed Smith by the belt and lifted, then began to drag him across the dirty plywood floor toward the door. As they left, he looked up and saw that several of the rafters were burning. A section of the roof over the stove at the back of the hootch fell in. Flames licked across the floor, and there was a series of small explosions as some of the canned foods blew up.

Outside again, Cavanaugh hauled the wounded men away from the burning team house, depositing them near the sandbags and protection of one of the other hootches. He managed to get Kepler to his feet and directed him toward Gerber's quarters. Anderson was semiconscious, unaware of the situation, mumbling something about the church service that should have ended ten minutes ago.

Then, near the dispensary, Cavanaugh saw a shape moving through the shadows and smoke of the burning buildings. He yelled, "Hey, Washington. Over here. Medic! There are wounded."

The man stopped, looked and then began moving toward him. Cavanaugh looked down at Anderson again. The big man seemed to be dazed but otherwise unhurt. There was no blood on his uniform, though it was torn, dirty and blackened where the fire had gotten too close.

When Washington arrived, his medical pack in hand, Cavanaugh ran back to where he had left Smith and picked him up. As he trotted toward Gerber's hootch, Smith over his shoulder in a fireman's carry, he noticed that the mortars and rockets had stopped falling. There was flickering light from the fires in the redoubt, but no one was trying to fight them.

IN THE FIRE CONTROL TOWER, Gerber abandoned the infrared scope and then the starlight because there seemed to be no ground assault coming. Through the eerie green light of the scope, the fields around the camp had appeared bare except for a single water buffalo that had escaped its pen. Using the huge binoculars that Kepler had stolen from the Navy, Novak studied the tree lines closest to the camp, searching for the origin of the flashes as the mortars fired or of the flames as the engines of the rockets ignited.

To the west Novak caught a flash. Turning and leaning forward so that his elbows rested on the sandbags stacked outside the FCT, he studied it and then pointed. "I've got one tube spotted, Captain."

Holding a field phone handset to either side of his head, he called for illumination to the west of the camp, but that only confirmed what Gerber already knew. It was a harassment mortar and rocket attack. He heard a loud, shuddering whir followed by a sharp, distinct crump as a mortar hit near the base of the commo bunker, throwing up a cloud of dust and smoke as it exploded.

Novak called out a couple of numbers, giving Gerber the range and direction of one of the enemy firing positions. Gerber relayed the message to the 81 mm mortar pits, ordering them to fire smoke rounds first. The white phosphorus exploded into spectacular fountains of flame easily visible from the fire control tower. Gerber adjusted for the pits until the rounds were dropping around the enemy's mortar positions. He then turned his attention to the destruction in his own camp.

Inside the redoubt he could see that the team house and dispensary were burning brightly, the flames shooting forty feet into the air. Beyond that a couple of the hootches used by the Vietnamese strikers had been hit, the black holes in the tin roofs evidence of the mortar damage.

Gerber spun the crank on one of the field phones. "Bocker, get a team together to fight the fires in the redoubt."

"Yes, sir."

"Greg, I want you to remain here and keep your eyes open. Charlie might be humping his tubes to new locations before dumping a few more rounds on us. I'm going down to help fight the fires."

"Yes, sir."

Gerber climbed over the sandbags so that he stood on the top rung of the ladder with his chest and shoulders still visible above the sandbags. "See if you can get a muster and damage report. You might have to coordinate a medevac."

"Yes, sir. I understand."

With that Gerber scrambled down the ladder and ran around the outside of the redoubt until he reached the entrance. He stopped for a moment and watched as a group of men, mainly Vietnamese strikers, used their entrenching tools to throw dirt into the fire. Others were running around the burning buildings, darting forward and then retreating as the heat became too intense for them.

Tyme had run out to the helipad and retrieved one of the large fire extinguishers, a huge metal tube on two big spoked wheels, and had pushed it close to the dispensary. The wide foam spray seemed to be smothering some of the flames.

Gerber saw Washington leave his hootch. He ran over to the medical specialist. "What's the status?"

"We've got Smith, Anderson and Kepler wounded. None of them seriously, but I want to get them evaced out of here." He nodded at the dispensary. "Especially since most of my medicine went up in flames."

"How about the Vietnamese?"

"Cavanaugh found one striker sitting on the ground and got him out of the field of fire. Few shrapnel cuts and a little dazed, but he should be okay."

"Any reports from the strikers' hootches?"

"Not yet."

Gerber left Washington and started for his hootch. He saw Cavanaugh sitting on the ground, his back to the sandbags, his hands clasped between his knees. The sergeant was staring at the dirt in front of him.

"You okay, Sean?" Gerber asked.

"I'm fine, Captain," said Cavanaugh, getting to his feet. "Just resting."

Gerber turned and looked at the team house as the roof fell in. The flames were fanned outward, and there was an explosion of sparks that shot into the sky. "Damn," he said. "Just convinced Crinshaw and his accountants in Saigon that we needed new furniture for the team house, got it out here and then Charlie burns it up."

"Yes, sir," said Cavanaugh.

Gerber looked at the young man, shrugged and entered his hootch. He saw Anderson sitting on the floor, Kepler in one of the chairs and Smith lying on the cot. "How are you guys doing?" he asked.

Kepler glanced at the others. "We're fine, Captain. That rocket caught us in the team house."

"How'd you get out?"

"Cavanaugh pulled us out. All of us. Ran in and out of the fire to get us."

"Jesus," said Gerber. "I saw him outside, and he didn't say a thing about it."

"Yeah, well, I've been sitting here thinking about it," said Kepler. "I was thinking that maybe we ought to put him in for the Silver Star on this one. Get the medal that he deserved the last time."

Gerber moved to his desk and leaned over it, pulling open the bottom drawer so that he could get at the bottle of Beam's. There was some shrapnel damage to his hootch—holes in the roof and in the metal wall locker, and his lantern was broken—but the bottle was intact. He jerked the cork free, took a swig and handed it to Kepler.

"I think," said Gerber, "that the Soldier's Medal might be more appropriate. We weren't really under attack, and he didn't have to fight off an enemy force to get into the team house."

"Yes, sir," Kepler said, "but Charlie was dropping mortars on us, and the Silver Star is the higher award." He handed the bottle back to the captain.

Gerber glanced at Anderson, who shook his head. "I'm trying to anticipate problems with the paper pushers in Saigon. The Silver Star might fly, but I think we'll have a better chance of getting him a Soldier's Medal. I don't want to get it downgraded on a technicality."

"That's the last thing we want," said Kepler. "Especially after what happened last time. Fucking brass hats." He looked up at Gerber. "You mind if I take another hit off that bottle?"

Gerber handed it to him, thinking about the discussion he had had with Fetterman about Cavanaugh drinking too much. Gerber shook his head. First thing he did after the attack was get a drink, and the second thing he did was share it. Maybe he was turning the whole team into a bunch of alcoholics. He watched Kepler tip the bottle to his lips and begin to chug the booze. Kepler swallowed several mouthfuls without breathing, lowered the bottle and said, "Yeah, that's smooth."

"Maybe you'd better go a little easy on that," said Gerber.

"Your supply running low?" Kepler asked.

Before he could answer, Novak appeared at the door. "Got a chopper coming in to evac the wounded, Captain. No one in the Vietnamese area was hurt badly. Just a couple of scratches that their medics patched up."

"Anything else?"

"Noticed some flashes near Cai Cai. Couldn't tell much about them though. Might have been grenades detonating or some kind of big fire. I thought maybe we should send out a patrol to see what's happening."

Gerber looked at his watch. "Let's wait for first light. I don't want to put anyone into the field tonight. Nothing they could do until morning, anyway, and a couple of hours won't hurt one way or the other."

"Yes, sir. Just a thought."

4

THE RICE PADDIES WEST
OF CAMP A-555

As the sun came up threatening another hot day, Cavanaugh
led his patrol of twenty-five Vietnamese strikers through the
gate, then turned toward the village of Cai Cai, which was now
marked by a towering plume of black smoke. They had crossed
the runway before the peta-prime had a chance to soften in the
sun, traversing the field of elephant grass. Mist hugged the
depressions in the fields, seemed to bubble from the streams
or riverbeds and clung to the trees and along the edges of the
swamps.

Cavanaugh kept the pace brisk, skirting the swampy areas
and avoiding the jungles by using the dikes in the paddy fields.
Normally he would have avoided the dikes, preferring to walk
through the paddies themselves, stepping on the young plants
to keep his feet from sinking into the dirty, feces-laden water,
but they were in a hurry. Airlift, in this case, couldn't be provided in the time it would take Cavanaugh and his men to walk
the twelve klicks to the village. The point man and the slack
were watching the path on the dikes carefully, looking for trip
wires and depressions that suggested booby traps. In this area

the farmers usually removed them as quickly as the VC constructed them.

They moved swiftly through the fields, staying as far as possible from the tree lines and the jungle. The patrol crossed unused roads, one of which had been paved in the past but was now broken with jagged pieces of slowly disintegrating concrete. They reached a hamlet of hootches with rotting thatched roofs, decaying fences of woven branches and degenerating wells and water buffalo pens. There Cavanaugh gave the signal to stop and spread out. The group began looking for signs that the VC had been there but found nothing. Fifteen minutes later Cavanaugh had them on their feet again, moving toward Cai Cai.

By midmorning the sun was bright, almost directly overhead in a cloudless sky. The heat radiated down to sap their strength, making them sweat heavily until their uniforms were soaked. The patrol began to slow. The pace decreased to a crawl, each step becoming an ordeal as they chased the column of black smoke that seemed to recede in the distance.

They continued, staying away from the trees, walking on the rice paddy dikes until the fields ended and the elephant grass began again. Fingers of jungle reached out from the Cambodian border and along the canals that crisscrossed the area. Cavanaugh avoided them, moving ever closer to Cai Cai.

Finally they walked into a narrow tree line, spreading out almost on line and then regrouping as they neared the edge. The point man crouched just inside the line of trees. The open ground in front of him was as flat and smooth as a blanket spread for a picnic. Cavanaugh crept toward him, using the cover of the bushes and trunks of the coconuts and palms and the shadows cast by them. He could see the village now but not the inhabitants. For several minutes he remained motionless, his eyes sweeping the remains of the hootches closest to him.

Cavanaugh and his men advanced on the village of Cai Cai, emerging from the trees and into the rutted streets that ran among the burned and smoking hootches. Some of them, constructed of mud walls and tin roofs, showed little evidence of fire. Others, made of thatch, were little more than smoking piles of rubble, and still others were gutted, the roofs missing and a wall or two tumbled into the interior. There were no people near the structures and no bodies among them.

They swept through half the village, checking the hootches, the remains of bunkers hidden behind or beside them. All they found were some dead pigs and chickens. It was as if everything that had any value had been removed and the rest, which couldn't be carried or driven, burned.

On the outskirts of the hamlet, they turned and started back, each of them silent now. Cavanaugh knew that a few of the PF strikers had families who lived in Cai Cai, friends who worked the rice fields and tended the pigs. The strikers were now worried. The villagers, seeing a large group of armed men approach, might take refuge at first, but once the identity of the men was established, they should have come out of hiding.

Cavanaugh stood at the center of the formation, the men spread out on either side of him, looking back toward the west, searching the side of the village they had yet to enter. At the far end was a large communal structure where the villagers congregated during the long summer evenings. A great deal of smoke was pouring from that area, and Cavanaugh was afraid of what he might find there.

Again they began their sweep, finding no evidence of the VC, except for the destruction of the village. On the mud walls of some of the hootches were pockmarks of rifle and machine gun bullets and scars of shrapnel from mortars and grenades. Cavanaugh stared at that and realized that the attack on Camp A-555 the night before had been a diversion for the real assault here.

As they moved through that sector of the village, they found the real horror. At first it was a single body of a village elder who had been shot, his blood staining the red dust a rusty color. His shirt had been stripped from his chest so that several bullet holes were easily visible. His black shorts, soaked with blood that had not yet dried, clung to his skinny legs.

The men moved slowly toward the fence of woven branches that surrounded the communal building. Lying near the gate was another corpse, one hand missing and most of the head gone so that the brain, a gray mass, had slid to the dirt. Wisps of smoke curled up from the shirt.

Almost as if someone had issued a command, the patrol hesitated. There was a rattling of equipment as the men checked their weapons and fixed their bayonets. It wasn't something that had to be done but something to do to put off the discovery they were about to make. Each of them knew what they would find; the stench being blown at them by the light breeze told them that the villagers had died the night before.

Inside the fence they found the rest of the villagers. Every man, woman and child was there, in some places their bodies heaped in piles. Most of them were charred, and Cavanaugh guessed that the Vietcong had tried to destroy the evidence. Some had obviously tried to run and had been cut down by rifle fire. Those bodies were riddled with bullet holes.

One of the PFs turned his head and threw up violently. He looked up at Cavanaugh, his eyes filled with tears, then was sick again.

Washington approached, holding out his medical bag as if it contained poisonous snakes and he was afraid that it might touch his body. "Christ," he said. "Jesus Christ."

Cavanaugh turned and stared at him, then closed his eyes, his face suddenly pale. He clenched his teeth, trying to suppress a scream of fury bubbling in his throat. He pulled the trigger on his weapon, firing the whole clip on automatic into the mud wall of the closest hootch. When it ran dry and the bolt locked back, he threw the weapon up, one hand on the butt, the other on the hot barrel. He ignored the pain, the cords in his arms standing out. He shouted something unintelligible and then kicked at the brass shells near his feet. He stomped them into the dirt, shouting, screaming, the rage etched on his face as the men stood there watching him, unbelieving and uncomprehending.

Finally he dropped to his knees and whispered, "Why, why, why?" until he saw that the others were staring at him. Slowly he rose and said, "Let's check the bodies. We don't want to overlook someone who might only be wounded." He stood quietly for a moment, waiting for them to react, and then added forcefully, "Let's move it."

Washington came forward. "I don't think there are any survivors. That's why they burned the bodies, to make sure. I'll get onto graves registration and make the arrangements there."

"You know what to do, T.J.," Cavanaugh said. "I'll take half the men and make another sweep through the ville to see if there's anything we might have missed while you do your thing here."

Without a word Washington turned and waved at the RTO. "Over here," he said. The medic then pointed at four of the strikers who were standing at the fence, their faces blank, looking at the smoldering bodies on the ground in front of them.

Cavanaugh stared at the scene for a moment, felt the hate begin burning in his gut again, a physical pain almost intense enough to make him cry out. His vision clouded, a black mass blocking the bright sun, giving the scene in front of him the black and white, grainy look of an old photograph. He clamped his teeth together and breathed through his mouth, trying to rein in his emotions as the bodies of the villagers shimmered and seemed to vanish, to be replaced by the strikers in the listening post and the field of dead Vietcong and NVA soldiers.

He turned slowly, dragging his eyes from the scene until he was looking at the tree line filled with coconuts, teak and palm, the huge broad leaves fluttering in the breeze. He felt extremely hot, sweat pouring from him, and his breathing became suddenly shallow and rapid. Gradually he became aware of his surroundings, the strikers standing near him, staring at him but afraid to speak.

"All right," he growled, trying to mask his emotions, "let's move out now. Search everything thoroughly."

With that he moved along the side of the village where the edge of a canal almost abutted the front of a hootch. The roof was gone, the remains a pile of smoking black debris. Cavanaugh pushed through the door, moving carefully, avoiding the hot spot. He found nothing. Everything of value had either been removed or burned in the fire. He pressed back to the rear and found the hidden entrance to a bunker but was reluctant to pry the top off. He forced himself to do it, even though he was afraid of what he might find there.

It was empty.

For the next hour Cavanaugh and the strikers searched the village. They found more evidence of the VC attack. There was an unexploded mortar shell buried nearly to its tail fins in the dirt. There were casings from AK-47s, the 7.62 mm shell shorter than the American-made version. Someone found a couple of unexploded Chicom grenades lying in the dirt near hootches.

The VC had evidently murdered some of the people in their hootches. Tracks on the ground showed where people had been dragged, and dirty ragged stains on the unburned bamboo mats showed where the wounded and dying had fallen. Clearly the VC had swept into the village for the sole purpose of killing everyone there.

As they completed their second search, Cavanaugh heard the sound of helicopters in the distance and turned to see a flight of Hueys swooping out of the sky. Washington, who was standing near the communal area, moved toward the open field to the west and tossed a purple smoke grenade into the grass. For an instant the breeze took the smoke, blowing it down into the grass, and then a large violet cloud blossomed.

Cavanaugh stepped to the safety of a standing wall of a hootch as the helicopters touched down, the lead ship putting its nose in the middle of the purple cloud. The rotor blades kicked up a whirlwind of dust and swirling grass. Nine other choppers followed, each one sliding to the ground in a staggered trail formation. As each of the helicopters landed, men leaped from the cargo compartments, crouching in the grass, their weapons pointed outward. They waited until the aircraft lifted off, climbing out.

The men from the choppers got to their feet, formed on line and began the short walk into the village, their weapons ready, their heads swiveling back and forth. Cavanaugh headed toward Washington. The sergeant noticed that the big medic was sweating profusely, his fatigues stained a darker color now. He had taken off his green beret, and the perspiration glistened in the curly black hair.

"Called in relief," he said when he saw Cavanaugh approaching. "Hell, there was nothing I could do. Too many people. Way too many. We've got to make sure that everyone gets a decent burial."

Cavanaugh nodded. Washington didn't have to explain it to him. The religion of the people demanded that they be buried, although he wasn't sure how much good it would do. Some of them believed that losing the head forced the deceased to wander the Earth for eternity. That was why the VC sometimes decapitated their victims. Maybe burning away the face did the same thing, Cavanaugh thought. Maybe these people would all be forced to wander the Earth. It was a terrorist tactic directed against the Special Forces camp and the Vietnamese who sought shelter in it.

The new arrivals from the helicopters worked their way across the open grass. Cavanaugh identified the commander by the RTO, who was sticking close to him. The man took the handset, halted and knelt. He snapped his fingers and pointed. Another soldier approached carrying a map and set it in front of the commander. Cavanaugh grinned, thinking that if he was a VC sniper, he could take out the entire group with a couple of well-placed rounds or a single grenade.

Finally the leader gave the handset back to the RTO, stood and folded his map, then handed it back to his sergeant. The line moved forward again into the village. Washington began angling toward the command party. He halted, waited and then turned to walk with them as the new force entered Cai Cai.

Cavanaugh moved toward them, falling in close enough to hear them but staying far enough away so that he wasn't part of the command party, just in case.

"What you want is graves registration," the young lieutenant was saying. "We're a line company."

"Yes, sir, and that is what I requested. But we need someone to stay here until the graves people can get out and take care of it."

The lieutenant stopped walking and turned to stare at Washington. "You want my men to guard a bunch of dead bodies? Bodies already mutilated by the VC? To make sure that the VC don't come back and do more damage?"

"Yes, sir. In a nutshell."

"You're out of your fucking mind, Sergeant. I don't give a good goddamn about what these slopes think. We'd be better off burning everything to the ground and paving it. The whole fucking country. Make it the world's largest parking lot."

Washington shot a glance at Cavanaugh and raised his eyebrows, but to the lieutenant he said, "Sir, it's important that we attend to this matter properly. Our strikers won't support us if we don't take care of this, and that means that an all-American camp will have to be built. Better four hundred strikers out here than four hundred Americans.''

The lieutenant unsnapped the straps of his helmet so that they hung down along his face. He rubbed a hand over his clean-shaven chin and said, ''We'll stay the night only because our CO told us to. Tomorrow we're out of here. Now what's the tactical situation?''

Quickly Washington began telling the lieutenant what they had found, using the map that one of the sergeants held out. While that was going on, Cavanaugh walked back toward the communal building.

Washington and his strikers had arranged the bodies so that they were in neat rows along the fence. He had covered the corpses of the children with the poncho liners taken from the strikers, but there weren't enough to cover all the bodies.

Cavanaugh looked at the line of dead. He had seen the same thing a dozen times. After every battle there were lines of dead, and it always seemed more horrible than bodies scattered over the field or lying in the wire or spread among the bunkers. Seeing them lined up for tallying and identification seemed to be the true sign that the people were dead. It was the final act before they were stuck in the ground to disappear from sight forever.

With a trembling hand Cavanaugh reached into the tunic pocket of one of his strikers and took a cigarette. The sergeant didn't smoke, but for some reason he felt the need to now. The striker just smiled at him, exposing a gap in his mouth where his three bottom teeth should have been. He produced an American Zippo lighter with the crest of the First Cavalry Division on it.

Cavanaugh let the man light the cigarette and cupped his hands over those of the Vietnamese as he sucked the smoke into his mouth and into his lungs. He grimaced and coughed violently, bending over with his eyes closed and the cigarette clutched in his left hand. He straightened, wiped the tears from his eyes and smiled sheepishly at the Vietnamese. Then the sergeant sat down, his back against the woven fence and watched the thunderheads building to the west. A shadow fell across him, and he glanced up to see Washington standing there.

"We can pull out now," said the medical specialist. "If you've seen everything you need to see."

Cavanaugh climbed to his feet. "I've seen more than I care to."

"Yeah." Washington stood there for a moment looking at the younger man and then asked, "You okay?"

"Fine." Cavanaugh smiled and dropped his cigarette, grinding it out with more force than necessary. "If you're referring to that little episode earlier, it was just seeing the way the VC treated the villagers. Rage that humans could do that to other humans. A momentary thing. It won't happen again."

Washington nodded, about to say something, then changed his mind. "Okay, then, let's get out of here. I've arranged to leave four of our strikers behind to help and act as scouts. They'll return to camp tomorrow."

"All right." Cavanaugh turned, waving an arm over his head to signal his men. Once they had gathered, they formed a line and began to work their way out of the village and back into the thick grass of the open fields.

They reached the camp about dusk, having stopped once to eat and once for a break. They had walked through most of the afternoon's heat, but as evening approached, the clouds appeared, blotting out the sun. A breeze from Cambodia picked up, blowing away the stifling humidity. They made good time after that, and with the camp as the destination, the men didn't try to think of ways to slow down. They wanted to reach it before dark.

As usual, Gerber met them as they entered the camp. He was sitting on the sandbagged wall, and didn't move as the group arrived, waiting for them to come to him. Washington turned, held his rifle over his head and said, "Weapons check in fifteen minutes. Get them cleaned, and then we'll get a hot meal."

As Cavanaugh approached, Gerber asked, "How bad was it?"

"Really grim, Captain. The VC either killed or carted away every living thing. We found some dead chickens and pigs, but I think the VC took most of them." He hesitated, as if unsure of what he should say next. "There weren't that many young girls around. I think the VC took them, too. Maybe some of the boys."

"Okay, Sean, write a report of everything you witnessed out there and any recommendations that you might have. Don't bust your butt on it, but I'd like it in the next two or three days."

"Yes, sir."

Cavanaugh turned to go, but Gerber stopped him. "How you doing?"

"Fine." He shrugged. "That was quite a sight out there, but I'm fine."

"Okay, Sean. See you later."

After Cavanaugh left, Washington stepped away from the Vietnamese strikers. He held his weapon in one hand and his medic bag in the other. "Captain," he said as he moved closer, "I've got to talk to you about Sean."

"Okay. Let's go to my hootch and you can tell me about it."

They crossed the compound, entered the redoubt and turned toward Gerber's hootch, passing the remains of the team house. The charred debris had been carted away. The concrete slab that formed the foundation of the structure had been cleaned and looked almost pristine in the fading rays of the dying sun. A new stack of plywood and a bundle of studs sat near the slab waiting for reconstruction of the team house to begin.

They entered Gerber's hootch. Washington noticed blood stains on the floor where the wounded men had waited to be evaced that morning. An odor of smoke hung in the air, and the screen above the bunk and over the desk was discolored from the fire in the team house. Gerber gestured at the metal chair and then slipped into his own. Without thinking, he reached for the bottom drawer where the bottle of Beam's was stored and then froze. Maybe they all were hitting the booze a little too heavily. He hadn't really thought about it until Fetterman had mentioned it, but maybe it was time to rethink some of their rituals.

"Okay, T.J., what's on your mind?"

"I'm a little worried about Sean," Washington replied. "Worried that maybe he came back to us a little too soon."

"I would imagine that you have a reason for saying that."

"Yes, sir. First, let me say that I would never do anything to hurt Sean. But if he's—"

"Let's just assume," Gerber interrupted, "that none of us would do anything to hurt him. But we are a combat unit and there are other considerations."

Washington nodded. "Yes, sir." He went on to tell Gerber about the sudden emotional outburst he'd witnessed when they had discovered the dead villagers.

"Was he completely out of control?" asked Gerber. "Could you get through to him?"

"We didn't try, Captain. It was a quick thing, like being called out at home when you know you're safe. A sudden flare of blind anger that burns itself out quickly. It's just something you can't have on patrol."

Gerber stood up. "You're right, T.J. I'll talk to Sean about it. Thanks for letting me know."

Now Washington was on his feet. "No problem, Captain. I do have one other question, though."

"What's that?"

"Where do we eat with the team house gone?"

Gerber laughed. "Well, for tonight I'm afraid we're stuck with C-rations unless you want to eat in the strikers' mess. Minh has invited us to share his facilities until ours are repaired. Either option."

"Thanks, Captain."

"And I'll talk to Sean, but I don't think we've got a problem yet."

"I hope not."

5

SPECIAL FORCES CAMP
A-555

For nearly twenty minutes after Washington left, Gerber sat in his hootch, watching the last of the sunlight fade until he was wrapped in darkness. He didn't bother to turn on the lights, even after he heard the main camp generator start up, signaling that they had all the electric power they would need. Finally he stood and moved to the door, peering across the compound. The work to repair the dispensary had progressed well during the day, and all that really needed to be done was a restocking of the medical supplies. They had been lucky that the damage had turned out to be only superficial.

He stepped into the compound and walked over to Cavanaugh's hootch. He was going to knock, but decided to look inside first. Cavanaugh was sitting hunched over on his bunk, an open bottle of bourbon between his feet. He seemed to be studying it rather than drinking from it.

"Sean, you got a minute?" asked Gerber.

Cavanaugh turned toward the camp commander. "Sure. You want a snort?"

"You drink all that by yourself?"

"Oh, not tonight, sir," replied Cavanaugh, picking up the bottle. "I've had this for a couple of days."

Gerber entered the room fully and looked around, at the metal wall locker with the jungle fatigues hung in it and the dirty clothes and boots thrown into the bottom of it, at the two cots covered with mosquito netting, at the plywood walls covered with pictures torn from magazines. Most of those near Sully's bunk were scantily clad blondes and those near Cavanaugh's were Second World War airplanes. There was a Coleman lantern sitting on a metal folding chair throwing its harsh white light into the room.

"How'd the patrol go today?" asked Gerber.

"You already talked to T.J., so you know what we found," said Cavanaugh.

"Yes, that's true. But I wanted to talk to you about it, too. Get a second point of view."

Cavanaugh snatched the bottle from the floor and took a long pull. He set it down and stared at it. "Come on, Captain, you know what happened on the patrol. I'm sure T.J. told you that I got upset when we found the villagers. Christ, sir, what did he expect? What do any of you expect? We find fifty people butchered and the bodies burned for no apparent reason other than the terrorist tactics of a guerrilla war. Of course I was upset by it. But it was a quick thing."

Gerber nodded but didn't speak. He waited, watching Cavanaugh.

"I know what you're thinking. I know what you all think. You're just waiting for old Sean to flip out again. Waiting for me to go crazy so that you can get me out of here. You didn't want me to come back. I had to ask the doctors. Hell, you didn't get down to see me all that often."

Gerber reached out. "Maybe I will take a drink." As he got the bottle and thought about what he was going to say, he realized that Cavanaugh did have a point. Gerber had been going to say that they were in a war zone where they couldn't hop into the car for a spin down to Saigon to visit a sick friend. But he realized that it wasn't true. They could get rides to Saigon in any of the helicopters that visited the camp daily, and many of the men had been in and out of Saigon dozens of times while Cavanaugh was in the hospital. They could have made a greater effort to visit him.

Gerber shrugged. "You're right, Sean, we could have. But we did have other priorities. That's not an excuse, just a fact. And you might have had to ask to be reassigned here, but that was because of the doctors in Saigon and not anything we did out here. When Bates called to ask if I wanted you back, my answer was yes." He grinned. "Not to mention the fact that we're shorthanded. Even more so now."

"Yes, sir." Cavanaugh took the bottle back and drank from it.

"By the way, I've put you in for the Soldier's Medal for pulling Anderson, Smith and Kepler out of the fire. I think you'll get this one. The criteria say that saving a life is not the only requirement for the award. You saved three and did it during a mortar attack, risking your life. I should have said something about that to you earlier."

"The Soldier's Medal, huh?"

"That's right. It's more of a humanitarian award than a combat decoration, but it seemed more appropriate."

"Yes, sir. Thanks."

"Oh," said Gerber, "I'm sending Lieutenant Novak out on a patrol tomorrow to see if he can find the trail of the VC who hit the village and maybe ambush them. Since we are shorthanded, I wondered if you would mind going out again so soon."

"Oh, hell, Captain, today's patrol was just a stroll through the park. We left in the morning and got back this evening. It's no big deal."

"Then contact the lieutenant sometime this evening and see what he has in mind."

"Yes, sir. No problem."

Gerber got to his feet and stepped to the door. "Sean, if I haven't made it clear before now, let me say that we're all glad to have you back. Probably Smith, Anderson and Kepler more than the rest of us."

"Thank you, Captain. Thank you."

THE PATROL FORMED AT DAWN the next morning at the gate. Twenty Vietnamese strikers stood in a ragged line facing Lieutenant Greg Novak, the big American. He was six feet two and a half inches, weighed about two hundred and seventy-five pounds and had short, dark hair. Although he had shaved before leaving his hootch, he already had a five o'clock shadow. He sported a pistolero mustache, which was against Army regulations, but no one really cared. Next to the tiny Vietnamese, Novak, whose nickname was Animal, looked like a giant.

As Cavanaugh joined them, Novak said, "Equipment check. I plan to stay out two days, minimum."

Cavanaugh nodded and began moving down the line, examining the packs of the Vietnamese, making sure that they carried everything they were supposed to have. He knew that they sometimes threw away or left behind items they could see no reason to carry. Each striker had his small first-aid kit, spare ammo for squad automatic weapons and a couple of spare grenades for the two M-79s. Then Cavanaugh searched through their packs for their personal rations. He moved along the line quickly, also checking the weapons to make sure they were clean and in operating condition, and that each man had two or three canteens filled with water. Novak watched for a moment and then started at the other end to speed up the process.

As they prepared to move through the gate, Cavanaugh with the point man, Gerber appeared from the redoubt. He stopped at the entrance, one foot up on the sandbags, and waved at them. When Cavanaugh saw that he wasn't going to come any closer, he opened the flimsy gate and passed through it. They went down the short road that led to the airstrip, turned to the north, and walked around the end of the runway before turning to the west to enter the fields of elephant grass.

They moved quickly through the field, breaking new ground, avoiding the paths used by the other patrols. The point man was rotated frequently because of the backbreaking nature of leading the men through the elephant grass. With each step the point had to twist his foot to one side or the other, breaking the grass so that the man behind him would have a trail to follow. After only fifty or a hundred meters, the point man's ankles, calves and thighs ached with the strain.

They moved from the elephant grass into the rice fields, stringing out along the dikes, angling toward the tree lines to the south. There were a couple of clumps of trees, tall palms with broad leaves, huge coconuts and teak trees towering above the rest. Tucked in among the trees were farmers' hootches surrounded by pens for chickens or water buffalo and encircled by fences of woven branches, bamboo and elephant grass.

By midmorning, with the sun high overhead baking the ground and sapping the strength of the men, they moved from the open territory into the trees, following the long axis of the tree line and finally moving into a thick sliver of jungle that jutted south from the Parrot's Beak to the edge of the Plain of Reeds. They halted as the undergrowth became thicker, the wait-a-minute vines tugging at the clothes, arms and legs of the men. The point was using his machete to open a path through the worst of it, slowing the march. Soon they came to a game trail, a wide path through the thickest part of the jungle, and diverted to follow it, increasing their speed.

At noon Novak called a halt for lunch. The men scattered through the thinning jungle, each watching an area ahead of him as he ate cold C-rations or rice and fish heads, then washed it down with the tepid water from his canteen. The canopy wasn't an impenetrable green sea from either the ground or the air but a splotchy, incomplete roof that let huge patches of sunlight through.

Novak made a routine radio check, joking with Bocker about remaining in the camp's cool commo bunker sucking down frosty Cokes, and then advised him that the patrol would be veering farther south. The only evidence of movement they had found on the game trail was a huge pile of steaming excrement left during the recent passage of an elephant.

When the meal was finished, Novak and Cavanaugh got the men on their feet and pointed them to the south. It was more of the same, except that the jungle had taken on the humidity of a steam bath, and they could almost hear the vegetation baking in the sun. There was a low, quiet hissing, as if it had just rained, and curtains of light mist drifted in the deep shadows. But there was no hint of a breeze that would provide a little relief.

Around them they could hear the chattering of the monkeys, the screeches and cries of the birds and the rustling of the tiny plants as small mammals ran through the jungle. They only saw one snake, a huge, brightly colored reptile that was draped over a branch split from a lightning-damaged tree, warming itself in the afternoon sun. They avoided it easily, none of the men wishing to disturb it.

Cavanaugh had just moved forward, passing several of the strikers as he tried to catch the point man, when he noticed suddenly the jungle was strangely quiet. He could still hear the hiss of the baking ground, but there were no longer the sounds of the animals that inhabited the area. Cavanaugh stopped to listen and then searched the canopy over him, looking for the movement of a monkey or the flash of bright color from the birds.

Puzzled now by the sudden lull, he crouched, one knee on the soft, wet ground. For an instant everything was suspended, the sound and motion of the jungle falling away into nothing—then the world seemed to blow up.

The first explosion was at the head of the patrol. Cavanaugh saw a geyser of dirt kick up near him and heard the scream of the point man as the shrapnel from the Chicom grenade tore into him. The sergeant dropped to the ground as more explosions ripped through the patrol. There was the staccato burst of a machine gun, and he could hear the bullets ripping through the foliage and smashing into the trees.

All around him there was shouting and shooting. The strikers were coming to life, returning fire now. Cavanaugh turned and saw the jungle floor littered with bodies, ten or twelve of his men down, their uniforms dark with blood. Then from the rear of the patrol came a roar like a lion gone berserk, and Cavanaugh saw Novak leap up and rush into the jungle, his M-16 blazing. He was bellowing, the words lost in the crash of the weapons and the explosions of the grenades.

The rest of the strikers were on their feet, running into the jungle, into the ambush, shooting from the hip, screaming at the tops of their voices. Cavanaugh, too, was up, racing off the trail and into the vegetation. He saw a flash of khaki hidden among the shadows and leaped for it. He landed next to an NVA soldier firing an AK at the bodies of the strikers. Cavanaugh slammed the butt of his rifle into the man's head and felt the enemy's skull splinter. He spun and dropped to one knee, his rifle against his shoulder.

For a moment he thought they had broken the back of the ambush. Then there was a bugle call from deeper in the jungle—a single searing note that built and dropped and was joined by whistles and shouts and renewed firing. A dozen enemy soldiers seemed to rise from the ground, coming at him. He fired once, saw the bullet hit, but the man kept coming, and he believed he was in one of his nightmares. His vision seemed to tunnel down until it was just him and the VC at opposite ends of a tube and everything else gone. Cavanaugh aimed carefully, pulled the trigger and saw the man's head disappear in a cloud of crimson as he fell to the jungle floor.

And then Cavanaugh was shouting, a scream erupting from his throat as he began pulling the trigger rapidly. He watched the enemy soldiers tumble into the jungle as his weapon kicked against his shoulder. Turning, he saw more VC and fired again and again, riddling them until the bolt locked back, the magazine empty.

As he hit the magazine release, dropping the empty clip to the jungle floor, he saw Novak rise, a VC in a headlock under each arm. A third rushed at him, but the lieutenant kicked out with a massive foot, catching the enemy soldier in the chest, knocking his rifle to the side and punting the man out of the way. He then slammed the heads together, smashing the skulls of the two VC. He dropped them, yanked his .45 from its holster and began firing at the enemy swarming around him.

Cavanaugh jammed a new magazine into his rifle, released the bolt to let it strip the first round into the chamber. He opened fire, trying to protect his lieutenant. An NVA regular materialized out of the bushes, weaving toward Novak, a machete held high in his hand. Cavanaugh aimed and fired, spinning him and dropping him as the machete flew back, flashing in the sunlight. The sergeant fired repeatedly, hitting enemy soldiers, but there were too many of them. Novak disappeared as they washed over him like a tidal wave. Then, miraculously, Novak was back on his feet. He picked up one of the VC and lifted him overhead, throwing him against the trunk of a teak tree. He grabbed another, one hand on each side of the man's head, snatching him clear of the ground. Suddenly Novak twisted the VC's head, snapping the neck with a popping noise that seemed to penetrate the sound of all the firing. The soldier went limp, and Novak dropped him.

Then Cavanaugh was busy, too, as the enemy rushed toward him from all sides. He emptied his weapon again, but before he could reload, a VC with a machete charged him. Cavanaugh grabbed the barrel of his rifle with his left hand, keeping his right hand near the butt. He thrust it forward to parry the chop as the VC tried to split his skull. The blade hit the rifle with a metallic clang and fell to the ground. Cavanaugh swung the butt around in a tight circle, clipping the VC just behind the ear. His eyes went blank as blood splattered everywhere. There was a crack as the stock of his M-14 shattered. Cavanaugh held it like an oversize pistol and tried to reload, but the enemy was coming too quickly. He then leaped out of the way, seeking cover momentarily behind the thick trunk of a palm. He worked the bolt of his damaged weapon, trying to reload.

To his right he saw Lieutenant Novak for the last time. The burly Special Forces officer was on his feet, punching at an NVA soldier. Novak hit him between the eyes, and as the soldier dropped, Novak suddenly staggered. Cavanaugh saw blood splash the front of the lieutenant's uniform, and then he stood straight up, roared and fell into the jungle.

Cavanaugh opened fire again, shooting at the VC and NVA who stood where Novak had been. He saw them topple over, thrown to the right and left, as his bullets slammed into them. Cavanaugh was grinning but didn't realize it. It was relief. Relief that his weapon was working as it should. Relief that the enemy wasn't able to avoid the effect of his bullets. He kept firing at them until his rifle was empty once more and the bolt locked back, the barrel smoking.

He tossed the rifle aside, grabbed his pistol and began shooting at everything that moved. Another NVA soldier appeared, looked wildly about him, then tried to break for freedom. Using a two-handed grip, Cavanaugh fired five times at the man's retreating back. But he never wavered. Cavanaugh lost sight of him in the thick jungle vegetation.

He spun then, searching for targets, but his surroundings were quiet. He turned slowly, but there was no one moving near him. He could see bodies lying on the trail among the trees and bushes and scattered along the jungle floor. From somewhere he heard a quiet moaning of a wounded soldier that ended suddenly. He crouched, felt the throat of the enemy soldier at his feet, but there was no pulse. On closer scrutiny he saw that most of the man's head was missing.

Slowly he moved through the trees, checking the bodies, searching for survivors. He found the lieutenant lying face-down in a pile of enemy corpses. Novak had been shot eight or nine times through the chest and stomach. One slug had ripped through his cheek to expose his teeth and gums. Cavanaugh checked him carefully, knowing that any of several of the wounds could have been fatal and that Novak was dead. But still the sergeant hoped that the lieutenant had somehow survived. Cavanaugh took the lieutenant's big combat knife, which Novak had bought at Ironmonger Jim's before he left the World for Vietnam. He fastened it to his pistol belt and said, "You got a lot of them, sir."

Cavanaugh surveyed the whole field of battle. He stopped counting the enemy dead when he reached fifty-two. Slowly he began to collect some of the weapons, then dropped them at the foot of a large, smooth teak tree near the trail. The strikers were all dead, too. Almost every one of them had been shot four or five times, and those who died on the trail were riddled with AK bullets.

Cavanaugh stumbled upon the RTO's body. Blood was still leaking from the half dozen or so slugs that had taken his life. The bloodstained radio was useless, having been shot to pieces. The RTO had died gripping the handset, and Cavanaugh wondered if he had lived long enough to get off a distress call. The smaller backup unit, the URC-10—little more than a hand-held survival radio—was missing. Cavanaugh searched the area near Novak's body for it after he discovered the larger radio was ruined, but couldn't find it.

Finally he gave up. He took one of the M-14s from a dead striker, moved away from the ambush site and sat down on the trail to wait. He wasn't sure what he was waiting for, but he knew that something would happen soon.

AT THE SAME TIME the patrol was being ambushed, Sergeant Galvin Bocker was sitting in the commo bunker, his feet propped on the OD green plywood counter. He didn't mind sitting in the dimly lighted, cool bunker while the rest of the team humped through the bush or worked on building the new team house. Monitoring the radios today, as always, was easy duty. Suddenly he caught a burst of static and a shout in Vietnamese over the Fox Mike. The yell was nearly drowned out by firing in the background, then all transmission was abruptly cut off.

Bocker leaped to the radio, grabbed the mike and tried to raise the patrol, assuming that they were in trouble. ''Zulu Five, Zulu Five, this is Zulu Base.''

He waited, not wanting to cut out their signal if they broadcast, but the sudden silence suggested that the radio had been destroyed. He waited a moment longer, heard nothing, made a last attempt to raise them and then raced from the commo bunker, heading for Gerber's hootch.

As he entered the redoubt, he saw the captain standing with Fetterman near the remains of the team house, the two of them talking to a couple of the Vietnamese who were helping to rebuild the structure. He called out, ''Captain, can I talk to you for a moment?''

Gerber turned, waved at Bocker and then told Fetterman, ''I'll get back to you.'' He moved to Bocker and asked, ''What is it?''

Bocker looked around, saw that no one was near and said quietly, ''I think our patrol has been ambushed.''

''You try to confirm?'' asked Gerber.

''I couldn't raise them. Thought I should brief you.''

''You try to get them on the Uniform? Novak had one of those URC-10s with him.''

"No, sir. I thought I'd better advise you."

"Okay, get back and try that. I'll let Tony know, and we'll be over in a couple of minutes."

"Yes, sir." Bocker turned and ran back to the commo bunker.

Gerber turned to face the team house. He called, "Tony, leave that and come over here." When Fetterman was close, Gerber said, "I think we've got trouble. You get a patrol together to see if you can find Novak."

"What is it?"

"I don't know. Get ready to move out and then meet me at the commo bunker. Make it fast and be prepared to leave in about fifteen minutes."

"Yes, sir," replied Fetterman. He headed for his hootch.

Gerber left the redoubt and entered the commo bunker. Bocker was sitting next to the rack of radios, using first the Fox Mike and then the Uniform, listening and trying again. Bocker's Vietnamese counterpart was standing behind the commo sergeant watching him work.

"You get anything, Galvin?" asked Gerber.

"No, sir. Just the one short call with all the shooting in the background and then nothing. The lieutenant might have the URC-10 turned off so we wouldn't be able to raise him, but we should be able to get him on the PRC-10. If something happened to that, I would think he'd be on the URC."

"What's the range on that?" asked Gerber.

"It's an ultrahigh frequency radio, sir, so we should be able to get something. Hell, on a good day you might be able to pick up a signal a hundred miles away. And if all else fails, he can always relay a message to us."

"He late on a check-in time?"

"Only about five or six minutes, but you know how that is."

Fetterman, wearing his field gear and carrying his M-3 grease gun, entered the commo bunker and walked over to the counter. "What's the word?"

"Not good. Can't get in touch with Lieutenant Novak." He glanced at Bocker. "Let's take a look at the map. Novak and I went over his patrol routes, so I think we should be able to find him."

They moved to the chart of the local area, which had been tacked to a piece of plywood then hung on the wall. Gerber studied it for a moment. "Given the time of day, I would guess that Novak should be in this area." He pointed and added, "Plans called for him to set up an ambush here, unless he found signs that the VC were moving elsewhere."

Fetterman nodded. "So if I come out the gate and turn southwest immediately, I can cut off a couple of klicks."

"That's right. He headed due west before turning south."

"Airlift, Captain?"

"We can try, but I don't think we can get anything out here fast enough to do us any good. Even if there was a unit available this late in the day, by the time they could get here and you loaded, you could walk to the jumping-off point."

"Yes, sir."

Gerber studied the map again. "You know, there are a couple of roads through there. If we loaded your patrol into the trucks, we could be into the area in half an hour."

"Tips our hand," said Fetterman.

"Seems that our hand's already been tipped." Gerber nodded. "Get your squad together, and I'll arrange with Minh to have them trucked out."

"Do we walk back?"

"No. We'll post a guard, and you can drive back once you get an answer. We'll establish a night laager on the road. A forward operating base for this."

"Pretty elaborate plan for something you're throwing together on the spur of the moment."

"Everything is in the manual. All we have to do is put the people into the plan and move out."

"Yes, sir."

THERE WERE four three-quarter-ton trucks and a jeep parked near the front gate. Thirty Vietnamese strikers were tossing boxes of C-rations, extra ammo and additional supplies into the trucks to be stored under the troop seats. Fetterman and Washington were loading medical supplies into the jeep. Mounted on the back was an AN/PRC-25 which would allow them to communicate both with the camp and every aviation unit in South Vietnam.

As Gerber approached, Fetterman broke off and walked over. "We're taking eight M-60 machine guns, a couple of mortars, lots of ammo for the M-79s and enough food to stay out a couple of days. Of course you can have anything else we need airlifted in."

"All right, Tony, you know what you're doing. Just report in every hour, and be careful because we don't know what happened to Lieutenant Novak and his patrol."

Fetterman turned and waved at Lieutenant Duc, who then ordered his men into the trucks. The drivers climbed into the cabs and started the engines. Washington and Duc got into the jeep and started it.

"Good luck, Tony."

"Thank you, Captain. See you tomorrow at the latest."

"Yeah, tomorrow." As soon as Fetterman got into the jeep, Washington spun the wheel, taking them through the gate. They drove along the edge of the runway, then south over a rough road before turning to the west along the path there that passed for a road. The vehicles kicked up a plume of dust that Gerber could see clearly from the gate.

As the dust finally settled in the west, he whispered, "Good luck, Tony."

6

WEST OF CAMP A-555
SOUTH OF THE
PARROT'S BEAK

Washington pulled the jeep onto an area of solid ground covered with elephant grass that jutted into the paddy fields. He leaned forward and turned off the engine, then sat up behind the wheel, his arm across the top of it as he stared at the trees about seventy-five meters ahead.

Fetterman was trying to locate landmarks on a map that was spread out on his knees. He glanced up and located the angle of the canal as it touched the road and then swung back to the west. There were a couple of black squares on his map labeled Numerous Hootches; farther to the west was a place of Strategic Hamlets. Fetterman folded the map. "Looks like we're as close as we can get on the road."

Lieutenant Duc hopped out of the back of the jeep. Reaching in, he retrieved his M-16, a bandolier of ammo and his pistol belt, which held two canteens and a tiny first-aid kit. He slipped the bandolier over his head so that it hung across his chest and turned to face the trucks that had pulled up behind the jeep.

The men began to jump from the trucks and were scattering; some of them chose to sit in the shade so that they were facing the rice fields where a single farmer was walking along behind his water buffalo. As they trod through the ankle-deep water, neither seemed to notice the trucks or the soldiers.

Fetterman climbed out of the jeep, picked up his weapon and started into the tree line.

"T.J.," he said, "let's take about ten guys and get moving. We'll sweep through on line, more or less, and see if we can pick up Lieutenant Novak's trail."

"I stay here," said Duc. "Have men set up perimeter and prepare the camp."

"Good," said Fetterman. He moved to the trucks, found a striker NCO and ordered him to pick nine others and get ready to move out. Squinting, he glanced at the sun, still high in the west, blazing in a blue sky. The storm clouds that had promised rain and cooler weather had blown away without releasing a drop of moisture. Now it was hot and humid, and without the wind in his face when the jeep had raced along the road, it was becoming miserable. Fetterman wiped the sweat from his forehead with the sleeve of his uniform.

The men assembled at the edge of the road, facing the trees, each with a pistol belt holding extra canteens and each with either a first-aid kit or additional medical supplies for Washington. They had two of the M-60 machine guns and ammo for it, and two men who were assigned as grenadiers carried the M-79s. Fetterman checked his map a final time, oriented himself with his compass and then stepped into the middle of the dusty road. He glanced over his shoulder, saw Washington follow, and then the Vietnamese. In seconds they were at the trees, where short elephant grass gave way to the dense jungle vegetation.

Fetterman pointed to the left and right so that the men would fan out and enter the jungle all at the same time. They swept forward slowly, some of the men needing to use a

machete to hack their way through the undergrowth, some of
them avoiding the huge trunks of the teak trees that reached
to a height of over a hundred feet. The rest dodged the small
thorny bushes or vines that snagged their fatigues and the
canvas of their equipment harnesses.

As they reached the center of the tree line where the vegetation was the thickest, masking the sky and the sun, they
found a game trail. Fetterman immediately noticed that
someone had used it recently. Fresh human footprints covered the soft ground, and he knew that they'd be quickly ob-
literated after dusk when the animals began using the trail. He
could see broken bits of grass or twigs and muddy spots where
men had stirred the decaying plants, exposing them to the air
for the first time.

Fetterman halted and whistled once, the signal that stopped
his men. They took up positions on either side of the trail, their
backs to each other so that they could watch the jungle all
around them. Fetterman moved to the south slowly, searching for evidence that the trail had been used for travel and not
just crossed. When he satisfied himself that he had found his
first clues about Lieutenant Novak, he waved the men to the
trail. Washington took up the rearguard position while he took
the point.

Before moving deeper into the jungle, Fetterman spread his
men out so that they were more than the five or six meters
apart, which was normal when patrolling. The game trail allowed them to see twenty or more meters ahead, and Fetterman didn't want the men walking into an ambush. When they
were set, he moved off, staying at the edge of the trail, using
the bushes, trees and shadows to conceal himself as he worked
his way to the south.

They stole forward, each man rolling his foot from heel to
toe to try to maintain stealth. No longer did they chop at the
vines and branches in the way, but ducked under them and
stepped around, pushing them only slightly and then easing

them back into position so that they wouldn't rustle. Each man was sweating heavily in the steamy jungle, his breath burning in his lungs as he tried to keep from panting at the exertion of moving quietly. It seemed as though cotton formed in their mouths and it was hard to swallow, but Fetterman had drilled them on the need for noise discipline and the need to ignore discomfort. They moved forward steadily, quietly, knowing that Fetterman would call a halt soon and let them drink their water, wipe the sweat and dirt from their faces and maybe even smoke a cigarette.

It was nearly five o'clock in the afternoon when Fetterman realized that he was getting close to something. The sounds of the jungle had changed slightly, as if the animals and birds had been chased away. He could see a slight blue haze drifting in the shafts of sunlight filtering through trees around him. An odor of cordite hung in the air, seeping toward him, warning him that a lot of weapons had been fired close by. Not a strong smell, just a hint of the acrid stink of gunpowder.

He halted the patrol and turned to watch them scatter from the trail, hiding in the foliage on either side. Then Fetterman crept forward until he could see the remains of a patrol through the gaps in the trees and bushes: ten or twelve men lying on the trail, their bodies shattered by the grenades and bullets of the VC, blood turning their uniforms rusty and staining the ground under them.

He saw Sean Cavanaugh sitting on a palm log, his back against the trunk of a teak tree, smoking a cigarette. He just sat there, his head swinging from side to side, as if he was watching a slow-motion tennis match, occasionally taking a puff of his smoke. There was a strange half grin on his face, as if he was in shock. Lying at his feet was the remains of his rifle, the stock broken and covered with blood.

Fetterman turned to the men behind him, pointed at one of them and then at his own feet, telling the striker that he was to move to the spot where Fetterman was crouched. As the patrol began to leapfrog slowly, silently forward, Fetterman stepped out onto the center of the trail where Cavanaugh would be able to see him easily.

When he heard the noise of Fetterman moving, Cavanaugh looked up, smiled broadly and waved. He laughed out loud. "The stupid bastards missed again. What took you guys so long? You missed all the fun." He stood up, flipped his cigarette into the jungle and laughed again. "Yup, you missed all the goddamned fun."

Fetterman noticed that Cavanaugh held a bloodstained pack of cigarettes in his hand, probably taken from the body of one of the strikers. Fetterman wasn't in a hurry because it appeared as if all the strikers on that patrol were dead. Each had been shot more than once. Limbs had been severed, and bits of white bone poked through bruised and bloody skin.

"They missed me again, Master Sergeant." Cavanaugh laughed. "If Charlie keeps this up, pretty soon the war will be over. He keeps throwing companies at me, and they keep failing."

Fetterman didn't speak. He pointed at his men and motioned them forward so that they could sweep into the jungle and routinely check the bodies to make sure that there were no wounded. He doubted that there were, but he wanted to be sure. He then moved closer to Cavanaugh, who stood empty-handed now, having stuffed the bloodied cigarettes into his pocket.

"Where's the lieutenant?" Fetterman asked.

"Over there somewhere," Cavanaugh said, pointing. He grinned, his face suddenly looking like a cheap mask pulled over a skull, then added, "He took a lot of them with him. Christ, it was fucking beautiful. Just slamming them together, killing them."

"Yeah," Fetterman said quietly. "You hurt?"

"Nah," said Cavanaugh. "I'm fine. Got a bunch of them, too."

"Okay, Sean, sit down and relax for a moment. We've got to look things over."

"Nothing to look over. The sons of bitches jumped us, and we shot our way clear, killing a boatload of them in the process."

"I see that," said Fetterman, "but I've got to check it out, anyway."

Cavanaugh sat down on the log again and fished a bloody cigarette out of his pocket. Fetterman turned away then, moving into the jungle, among the trees and bushes and rotting vegetation, looking at the bodies lying hidden there. Occasionally he scanned the faces of his strikers, observing the shock as they searched the battlefield. They were thinking and feeling the same thing that all men thought and felt as they walked a new battleground—relief that they weren't lying dead themselves, and betrayal that they had somehow let their friends and fellow soldiers down by not being there for the fight. Fetterman had long ago realized that he hadn't betrayed his friends by remaining alive when they died. He felt that he would only betray himself by dying before his time.

He found Lieutenant Novak lying facedown among a pile of enemy bodies, his right hand wrapped around an NVA sergeant's throat as if he had squeezed the life from the soldier as he was dying himself. His rifle lay empty near his feet, and his pistol had been fired until the slide locked back. Cavanaugh was right. The lieutenant had taken a lot of them with him.

When he returned to the trail, he saw Washington kneeling near Cavanaugh, looking into his eyes, his medical bag open beside him. "You check the others?" he asked when Washington noticed him.

"They're all dead," said Washington. "Every one of them. They've all been hit six, seven times, except one guy who had a little hole just above the right ear and Sean here. Sean is fine."

"Of course I am. Like I said, if Charlie keeps this up, the war will be over soon."

"That's enough, Sean," said Fetterman. "Looks like the war is already over for the lieutenant and the rest of the patrol."

"Lighten up, Master Sergeant. It's not my fault I lived through it. Looks like I'll get another medal, but I don't suppose it'll be the CMH for this one, either."

IT WAS DUSK BY THE TIME the patrol reached the trucks, each man carrying a couple of the weapons that had been found on the battle site. Duc had done what he had said he would, setting up a camp that commanded the road and the fields surrounding them. He had placed his machine guns to face the most likely routes of attack, leaving two spots empty so that Fetterman could add his two to the fields of fire. The trucks had been parked in the center of the perimeter, forming a makeshift redoubt in case the attack was too large to beat back easily.

As they approached, Fetterman saw that the rice farmer had given up for the day and was gone, but there was a wisp of smoke from a clump of trees two hundred meters away, suggesting that he and his family were there cooking their evening meal.

Duc left the front seat of the jeep where he had been sitting watching the sun, a flaming ball of orange that seemed to bounce on the horizon. He saw Cavanaugh and the look on the faces of the strikers. "You have found them?"

"We found them," said Fetterman. "They're all dead. I think we should get back to camp as soon as we can."

"I think we can be ready to go most ricky tic," Duc replied.

"I'm going to report," Fetterman said, more to Washington than to Duc. "See if the captain has any instructions for us."

Duc moved with Fetterman, dogging his heels. "Where are the others?" he asked. "You didn't leave them in the jungle?"

"For now, yes. No way we could bring them out. Have to mount an operation in the morning to get them."

"But Charlie come back and cut them."

"I don't think so, Lieutenant," Fetterman told him. "I don't think many of the VC survived the ambush, and I doubt they'll return tonight."

They had reached the jeep, and Fetterman grabbed the handset from the AN/PRC-25 mounted in the rear. "Zulu Base," he said, "this is Zulu Three."

"Ah, Three, this is Base. Go."

"Roger, Base," said Fetterman. "We have located the missing patrol and are prepared to come in."

"Understand you have located the patrol. Say condition."

"Condition is bad. Just about as bad as you can get."

"Understood. Can you wait one for Zulu Six?"

"Affirmative," answered Fetterman. He set the mike on top of the radio and stared to the west. He was remembering the last time he had come upon a scene like the one today. Cavanaugh had been sitting there quietly, clutching an E-tool that had dried blood all over it. He hadn't said a word to them. He had just stared into the foxhole where the RFs lay dead. His position had been surrounded by bodies then, too. Fetterman wasn't sure that Cavanaugh was handling it any better this time. His attitude was different but not really better.

The radio crackled, and a tinny voice spoke. "Three, this is Six. Understand that you want to come in?"

"Affirmative. No reason to remain in place this evening."

"Do you have wounded?"

"Negative. I have no wounded. Repeat. I have no wounded."

"Roger. Bring it on in, and report to me soonest."

"Roger, Six." Fetterman dropped the mike into the jeep. He looked at Duc. "Let's get out of here."

Within ten minutes they had broken camp and loaded the trucks. The convoy moved out, bouncing along a road now obscured with shadows as the last of the light faded. Fetterman didn't like using the same road, but he didn't think the VC would have a chance to get an ambush into place. They hadn't been out that long, and there was too much open ground. Even with the headlights on, shining through the rectangular slits that made them more difficult for the enemy to spot, Fetterman thought they were relatively safe. If they had stayed overnight, Charlie might be waiting, but not now. Not enough time.

Soon the camp came into view, and there was no way that Charlie would hit them. They drove along the runway and pushed through the gaps in the wire. As they passed through the gate, a squad rushed out to close the concertina over the road so that the rings of wire around the camp would be complete for the night.

Gerber was waiting as the trucks rolled to a halt. He confronted Fetterman and demanded, "What in the hell happened?" Then he saw Cavanaugh. "Sean? You all right?"

"Yes, sir. I'm fine. We got ambushed. We—"

Fetterman put a hand on his shoulder. "Captain, they were wiped out. Everyone, except Sean here. Lieutenant Novak is dead."

"Jesus Christ," said Gerber, stunned. "Jesus Christ." He put a hand to his forehead and asked again, "What happened?"

"I haven't debriefed Sean yet," said Fetterman. "They walked into it and, following procedure, charged the ambush and broke it up. I counted over fifty dead VC and NVA there. We brought in most of the weapons but had to leave the bodies. Figured we could get them in the morning. It'll be an all-day job, but we should be able to get them all before dusk tomorrow."

"Sean, how are you feeling?" asked Gerber.

"Just fine, Captain. Little hungry, but fine otherwise."

"T.J.," said Gerber, "want to oversee the cleaning of the weapons and storage of the captured stuff before grabbing some chow?"

"Sure, Captain."

"Tony, I want you and Sean to come over to my hootch and tell me exactly what happened. Sean, we haven't finished the team house yet, so we're still eating C-rations. We can get you some if you want."

Once in Gerber's hootch, they went over the details of the ambush. Between mouthfuls of C-rations, Cavanaugh told them about Novak's actions during the ambush and explained that the unit they ran into was company strength at the minimum, maybe even larger. He had seen no cowardice by anyone. Everyone had reacted quickly, but there had been too many VC.

For the next twenty minutes Gerber quizzed Cavanaugh on the battle and on how he felt. Cavanaugh explained that he hadn't liked sitting alone in the jungle, but given the circumstances, he didn't mind it all that much. He had felt that someone would come by soon.

Gerber tried to press him about his feelings, but Cavanaugh dodged the questions easily, giving flip answers and saying that it had all happened before. He finally asked Gerber if he was going to put the lieutenant in for a medal.

"Of course," Gerber replied. "He'll automatically get a Purple Heart, and I think we'll put him in for a Silver Star. He should get that. I think Minh will put the strikers in for a Cross of Gallantry or something like that. At least that's what I'll advise him."

"And me?" asked Cavanaugh.

"Well, Sean, given the circumstances, I doubt that we could get you the Medal of Honor. Hell, I think you deserve it, especially after the defense of the listening post, but we're stuck again. No witnesses to the action. Just the physical evidence scattered in the jungle. Hell, Sean, we'll try to get you a Distinguished Service Cross."

"Yes, sir! Thank you, sir!" The enthusiasm in his voice was unmistakable.

"Christ, Sean, you deserve it," Gerber repeated as he got to his feet. "Look, I know you've had a rough day. Why don't you hit the sack? We'll talk tomorrow."

"Yes, sir. Say, you get a report on how the others are? I mean Smith and Anderson and Kepler."

"They're all fine. Smith and Kepler might be able to return in a week or so. Sam has been evaced to Japan for treatment."

"Okay, sir." Cavanaugh turned and left.

"Tony," said Gerber, "what do you think?"

"About what?"

"Cavanaugh. You're the one who found him both times. What's your reaction?"

Fetterman rubbed his face as he thought. "He seems to be a little too emotionless this time. No real reaction from him. It's like he was lost in the jungle for a couple of minutes. He seems to be a little too flip."

"Better than being catatonic."

"Yes, sir, if you say so, though I'm not convinced that's true."

"What do you mean by that?"

"Simply that Cavanaugh may be a walking time bomb. I would have liked to see a little more emotion. After all, he had just witnessed his patrol being wiped out again."

"Maybe the difference is that he wasn't in charge this time."

"I think it's more than that. I think we better keep an eye on him for a couple of days."

"I had planned on that, Master Sergeant."

7

THE VIETNAMESE
QUARTERS, CAMP A-555

Cavanaugh exited Gerber's hootch, but rather than returning
to his own, he left the redoubt and turned toward the Vietnamese quarters. He shuffled around the compound, staring
at the small square hootches that accommodated eight strikers or that, sometimes, were divided into four rooms so that a
striker who had a family could have a little privacy.

The hootches were constructed along the lines of the Americans': there was a wooden frame, plywood halfway up the
walls, the top section screened in and the whole covered by a
corrugated tin roof. Most of the structures had been sandbagged, but a few had piles of sandbags in front of them, waiting for someone to stack them around the hootch. There were
wooden sidewalks between the hootches, one-by-twelves laid
on their edges with planks nailed to them. Wires were strung
everywhere, running from poles into the hootches to provide
electricity. The smell of nouc-mam was heavy in the air.

Cavanaugh wandered around, searching the faces of the
Vietnamese strikers who sat outside, wearing little more than
black shorts or their OD GI underwear, shower shoes in a riot
of color on their feet, and chattering with one another as the

discordant music from a Vietnamese radio station drifted on the light, warm breeze. One group he recognized as men who had either been with him at the village of Cai Cai or who had relatives in it. They were not talking or laughing. They had watched solemnly as Chinook helicopters flew the bodies of their relatives and friends from Cai Cai to be buried in the makeshift graveyard established north of the camp. In their hootches, they had erected little altars and burned incense on them, leaving small portions of food, such as boiled chicken, nouc-mam, fruit cocktail from American C-rations and rice, as an offering for the dead.

Without an invitation Cavanaugh sat with them. They had looked up as the American approached, not acknowledging him but not telling him to leave. They sat quietly for a while, staring at the night sky encrusted with stars and listening to the radio music.

Finally Cavanaugh said, "It's too bad we can't get even with the VC. They sneak in and kill innocent people and run to Cambodia to hide."

A couple of the strikers looked at him, but none of them spoke. They ignored his comment. One of them got to his feet and went into the hootch.

Cavanaugh watched the door for a moment and then looked at the men sitting with him. "We can get even." He waited and then added, "There is no reason for them to get away with their chicken shit tactics of killing the innocent and running away to Cambodia."

When no one spoke, he added, "We can go after them. Just a couple of us, moving at night through the jungle, waiting for them and killing them."

He looked at the impassive faces and wondered what they were thinking, how they were feeling. "You've seen what can be done. You know that the VC are not supermen. They are murderers who sneak through the night and prey on helpless women and children. They kill in a wanton fashion. They are dogs who should be hunted down and shot.''

None of the strikers spoke, but none of them left, either. Cavanaugh remained silent for a moment, waiting for what he said to sink in. Then he continued. ''We can't let them get away with it anymore. The brass hats in Saigon, both American and Vietnamese, don't understand what is happening out here. We do. We have to do something about it. Show Charlie that he is not safe here anymore and should stay in Cambodia. When he shows up here, we kill him. Quickly.''

''How soon?'' one of the strikers asked.

''Tomorrow. The next day. Soon.'' He smiled. ''You know that I'm invincible. You all know that. You've all seen the results of that.''

''What we do?''

''Okay,'' said Cavanaugh, clapping his hands together once. ''Okay, when Minh or whoever is trying to put together a patrol, you volunteer. We'll just go off and do our thing then.''

He looked at the six men there, men who had lost relatives in the VC raid at Cai Cai, Vietnamese strikers who weren't really soldiers but rice farmers and shopkeepers playing soldier. Men who sometimes closed their eyes when they fired their weapons, who liked to fire a whole magazine on full auto and then hug the ground until the shooting stopped.

But something new had been added. They had lost family and friends to the VC. The war was no longer something that happened in the next village or the next province. It was something that happened to them, might be the motivation they needed, if he handled it right.

''Okay,'' he repeated. ''We'll go looking for the bastards the first chance we get. You don't need to say anything to your officers or sergeants, I'll square it with them. Maybe we'll start with some extra rifle practice.''

He stood and looked down at them, vague shapes in the night. A little light from the hootches spilled out so that Cavanaugh could see the profiles of the men. He thought there was something else he should say to them but didn't know what it should be. He wasn't even sure that they understood what he had said to them. All he could do was try to form the core of a team that would go out to kill the Communists.

As he headed toward his hootch in the redoubt, he realized that he would need a top-notch NCO to work with him. He doubted that any of the other Special Forces sergeants would understand what he was doing. But Krung would. Krung was like the Vietnamese strikers. He had lost his family to the Vietcong and had sworn to kill fifty enemy soldiers for each member of his family. He would welcome the opportunity to go out hunting the VC. Cavanaugh decided to talk to Krung, then stopped short and smiled. He didn't need to talk to Krung. When the time came, Krung would be ready.

CAVANAUGH GOT his first chance the next day. Gerber had told them that a patrol would be sent out at first light. Cavanaugh volunteered for the mission, but Gerber told him that Tyme would be taking it out. Besides, Cavanaugh would be responsible for leading a company out to where the ambush had taken place.

At first he hadn't been happy, but then the American had realized that once he got into the field, he could take a patrol out to swing through the jungle as if he was looking for any VC who happened to be near. Once he was away from the main body, he could get permission from base to keep chasing the enemy if he happened to see them, and Cavanaugh knew that one way or another he would see them.

He watched Tyme's patrol walk through the west gate and cross the runway before turning north toward the jungle and the Parrot's Beak region. As they slipped from sight, the trucks that would carry his patrol into the field pulled up. The Vietnamese strikers were already loaded. They carried entrenching tools, body bags and lots of water. They also had their weapons with only a basic load of ammo, enough food for a noon meal and little else.

Cavanaugh checked on the six strikers he had talked to the night before and told them to get their full field gear and to carry enough to stay in the field for three days. As they ran off to get the rest of their equipment, Cavanaugh went to find Krung.

Twenty minutes later they were rolling out of the camp, trucks kicking up a cloud of dust as they turned onto the road that would take them to the jungle where the patrol had been ambushed. Cavanaugh rode in the lead jeep with the Vietnamese company commander. He had one foot propped up on the dashboard as the countryside rushed by. It didn't take them long to get to the place where Fetterman had stopped the trucks the day before. The Vietnamese lieutenant had them circle the trucks like the wagon master circling the Conestogas on the western plains. The men jumped out the backs and spread out, finding shade to relax in until someone told them what to do.

Cavanaugh left them alone while he got his private patrol ready, then advised the Vietnamese officer that they had better get going. Within minutes everyone, except a small detachment left to guard the trucks, was moving through the trees. Cavanaugh was on the point, leading them to the game trail and then along it until they had worked their way nearly to the spot where the ambush had taken place. He halted the column and crept back to the Vietnamese lieutenant.

"Sir," he said, "down this trail about fifty meters is the place where we were ambushed. I would like to take six of your men and Sergeant Krung and move through the jungle to the right of that position in case there's anybody still hiding in there."

The lieutenant nodded as if considering the advice and then said, "Very good. I lead men down trail and begin unhappy task of claiming bodies."

"Yes, sir. I would like to take one of the radios with me so that we can maintain radio contact with one another."

"That is good. You do that. I wait here for a while to let you move into position," the lieutenant told him.

Cavanaugh nodded and crawled off, pointing to the men of his hunter-killer team. He assembled them at the rear of the column, checked his map and then moved to the east, through what looked like the thickest part of the jungle. Cavanaugh began hacking at the dense undergrowth with his machete, creating a path for his men. Suddenly they popped into a clearing, a field of elephant grass that sloped gently to a group of rice paddies. Cavanaugh turned the men to the south, moving along the edge of the jungle just inside the trees until he was more than a klick from the ambush site.

He stopped around noon and set up a small perimeter so that the men could eat lunch. Then, before they moved, Cavanaugh used the radio.

"Zulu Base, this is Zulu One Two."

"One Two, this is Base. Go."

"Roger, Base, I have found evidence of VC and am pursuing in accordance with instructions from counterpart."

There was a hesitation and then, "Roger, One Two. Please advise Six on intentions in one hour."

Cavanaugh rogered the instruction, gave the handset back to the RTO and got his men to their feet. They stayed inside the tree line, moving rapidly farther south until they reached a swampy area where the jungle disappeared. Cavanaugh turned to the west again, moving deeper into the jungle, veering slightly to the north to avoid the mushy ground.

At midafternoon, when the sun was at its hottest, Cavanaugh halted his team. They infiltrated the trees, each man finding a good hiding spot. They had come to a trail, a path through the jungle whose width suggested that human beings had made it. It could have been farmers or VC. Cavanaugh decided that they would rest there for the afternoon, and if nothing happened by ten or eleven o'clock that night, he would think about redeploying them.

They passed a quiet afternoon, moving only to take a drink of water, their movements slow, easy and hard to see in the deep shadows and jungle vegetation. At dusk they ate cold C-rations, half of the group on guard while the others ate, then rotated the duty. As the sunlight faded, Cavanaugh moved them a hundred meters farther west in case someone had seen them during the day. Once they were settled, Cavanaugh instructed them that there would be no talking, no movement and no smoking. They were waiting for Charlie and didn't want to tip their hand.

As he settled in, Cavanaugh switched magazines in his rifle, putting in one that was all tracers. He set two hand grenades on the ground in front of him where they could be reached easily and placed a single star cluster flare next to them. Then he crouched, one knee on the ground so that he wouldn't relax too much. He wished now that he had brought a claymore mine or two but had figured taking any would draw attention to his plan.

A dozen things flashed through Cavanaugh's mind. When hunting ducks, you stayed in one place and waited patiently. But he didn't want to wait patiently, he wanted to kill the enemy. He knelt there, his rifle clutched in both hands, waiting, listening, knowing that it would be an hour at least before he could expect any VC. His training reminded him that he should alert the camp about his location and intentions, but he decided against it. The captain would be pissed, but if he ran up an impressive kill record, the captain would get over it.

Far to the right he heard something. A quiet snap and a voice speaking Vietnamese. Cavanaugh tensed, let his finger slide along the trigger guard of his M-14 to slip off the safety. A moment later there was a rustle in the bushes, then Cavanaugh saw a shape loom out of the darkness.

His first instinct was to hose the trail with his M-14, but the American realized quickly that such an action would only identify his location for the enemy. Instead, he reached for one of the grenades, pulled the pin, holding it in his left hand in case he wanted to replace it, and waited. The shape faded into the background again as more men approached. Finally he let the spoon fly, hesitated and then threw the grenade.

Hugging the ground, he watched through the trees as the grenade exploded in a fountain of sparks and flying shrapnel. A second later there was another explosion farther down the trail, followed by two more as the strikers lobbed their grenades. Cavanaugh poked his rifle forward, aimed at a point on the other side of the trail and opened fire, pouring the whole magazine into the shadows.

The enemy, surprised, reacted slowly. There was a shout and then a whistle. One man opened fire with his AK-47, the muzzle-flash extending three feet from the end of the barrel. Two grenades detonated beside him.

From the east another AK opened fire. Cavanaugh spun toward it, watching the bursts for a moment, then returned fire, aiming at the center of the muzzle-flashes. He squeezed off a quick burst, dodged to the right and waited. There was no return fire.

The jungle fell silent. Cavanaugh listened intently, his eyes flicking from shadow to shadow, searching for movement among them. After five minutes he moved cautiously to his right. He found Krung, and together they moved among the patrol, shifting them another hundred meters to the west again, in case Charlie had identified his location and tried a counter ambush.

Cavanaugh settled down with his back to a large palm tree. There was little vegetation in front of him, and he could see some shadows shifting and dancing near the trail. Slowly he raised his hand and wiped the sweat from his face. Even though the sun was long gone, the heat and the humidity remained. Cavanaugh breathed quietly, ignoring the weather and concentrating on his surroundings, memorizing the positions of the bushes and trees, watching the shadows, searching for any unnatural movement.

After an hour he realized that something had changed around him. He reached up, touched the hilt of the knife taped upside down to his shoulder harness, then felt along the trigger guard of his weapon, checking the safety. He heard a quiet rustling and turned toward the sound. Something was moving slowly through the shadows, along the side of the trail. A hand seemed to snake out, feel its way and then ease to the ground as the weight of the body behind it shifted forward.

The figure pulled even with him, only a few feet away. Cavanaugh rocked forward so that he was on his hands and knees, his eyes never leaving the form near the trail. He moved cautiously toward the enemy and when he was close, he set his rifle on the ground with the operating bolt upward to keep it clean.

Cavanaugh launched himself at the enemy, landing in the middle of his back. The man collapsed to the ground, the air forced from his lungs in an audible grunt. Cavanaugh's left hand shot out and grabbed the man under the chin, snapping his head back to expose the throat. There was a whisper of the knife against flesh that sounded like tearing silk. Cavanaugh felt the warm blood splash over his hand. The enemy bucked once as if he was trying to throw him off, and then the tension seemed to flow into the ground with the man's blood.

Cavanaugh rolled off his victim, scrambled back a pace or two and reached for his rifle. His hand touched the barrel, and he let his fingers ease along it until he felt the rear sight. He picked it up and checked the safety again, making sure it was still off.

Alerted by a sudden noise behind him, Cavanaugh turned around to see a man standing over him, holding his machete high as if preparing to swing it at a thick vine. Cavanaugh rolled onto his right elbow and fired without really aiming. The impact of the slug slammed the man backward, sending him into the dark shadows of the jungle.

At that moment Cavanaugh realized that he and his men were right on the infiltration route the VC were using to try to reclaim the bodies of the men killed in the first ambush. With the need to keep quiet, Cavanaugh had lost contact with his troops. He could only hold his ground, killing the enemy as he saw them moving. He no longer had any good idea of where his men were. If they had slipped from cover in search of VC, they could be scattered through the jungle. The integrity of the ambush was gone, and he was suddenly in as much danger from his own strikers as he was from the Vietcong. It was a mistake that could kill him.

But then he saw another enemy soldier crawling through the jungle. A single man dressed mostly in black, but wearing one of the khaki pith helmets that the NVA regulars favored. Cavanaugh didn't move, watching the soldier as he came closer. When he was three feet away, Cavanaugh reached out with his rifle, put the muzzle next to the soldier's head and, as he turned to look, pulled the trigger. The VC's body was hurled to the left into a bush, his head blown apart.

Off to his left he heard more movement. His men would be to his right, Cavanaugh guessed, reaching for another grenade. He pulled the pin and waited. Soon a rustling noise broke the silence, and he tossed the grenade in that direction, flattening himself behind the trunk of a fallen tree. He buried his face in the ground and closed his eyes to protect his night vision. Before looking up, he heard the explosion of two more grenades and recognized the flat bangs as the detonations of American weapons.

He heard a new sound in the trees as if someone had thrown a ball or a rock in the forest. It hit something solid, then fell, and a second later it exploded with a dull, subdued pop. It was then that Cavanaugh realized the VC had begun to chuck grenades at him.

For an instant he was consumed by fear. No longer was he the invincible Sean Cavanaugh, survivor of two bloody hand-to-hand fights, but the nineteen-year-old kid who should have been watching his classmates play football on Saturday afternoon. He shifted himself around so that he was lying parallel to the tree trunk and tried to force himself under it for protection. Pressing his face into the soggy, damp jungle floor, smelling the dirt and rotting vegetation, he wondered what the pain would be like if the white-hot shrapnel hit him.

Cavanaugh slipped deeper into cover and felt along his harness to see how many grenades he had left. During the action he'd forgotten how many he'd carried with him and how many he'd thrown. There were two left, and he decided not to use them unless a good target presented itself. Lying there, pressed up against the log, he turned his head so that he was facing the bottom of it, the odor of the damp jungle in his nostrils. The realization suddenly came to him that he was panting, as if he had just sprinted a hundred meters. He slowly moved, turning so that he could look into the jungle. It was alive with night sounds, and a light breeze rippled through the leaves. Tiny creatures scrambled for safety as they tried to flee the area, sensing the unwanted human presence.

By staring into the gloom, Cavanaugh could see the phosphorescence of rotting vegetation glowing among the deeper black of the shadows. His ears twitched as they picked up the quiet sounds around him, and then they were lost as the blood hammered through his veins and his heart pounded in his chest.

His fear evaporated slowly when he realized that the enemy didn't know where he was. Besides, they were using Chicom grenades, explosives so inferior that they didn't detonate half the time. When they did, they had very little force and almost no shrapnel. He remembered the Army captain he had met once who had been hit on the head by a Chicom grenade that detonated on impact, forcing the man's helmet down so that it had to be cut from his head. The captain had taken some shrapnel hits in the shoulders, but he should have been dead instead of in Saigon joking about the incident.

Cavanaugh rolled clear of the log and crawled backward, toward the tree where he had started. He crouched there for a moment and then lay down, flattening himself on the ground beside the tree. He stayed like that, listening and waiting for the enemy, but it seemed that the grenade duel was over and that the enemy had retreated.

After a long time Cavanaugh moved so that his left wrist was right under his eyes. He peeled the camouflage flap off the top of his watch so that he could check the time. It was nearly 4:00 a.m. The hour surprised him because he wasn't sure whether he expected it to be much later or much earlier.

Suddenly he was uncontrollably thirsty. Cavanaugh tried to tell himself that he didn't need a drink, but that didn't work. It was as if he could hear his body drying out, and his thoughts were focused only on the water in his canteens. He realized that the obsession with getting some water was worse than actually taking a drink. If he didn't, he wouldn't be able to pay attention to what was happening around him. Slowly he reached down and tugged gently at the snaps on the cover of his canteen. They pulled free with an audible pop, and Cavanaugh froze, but no one seemed to have noticed. Carefully he slipped the container out, unscrewed the top, and lifted it to his lips. At first he drank greedily, ignoring the plastic taste of the warm water. It dripped down his chin and onto his sweat-soaked and dirt-stained shirt. Finally he stopped, took a breath and then sipped the water, drinking it slowly until the canteen was empty. Rather than fumble with it further, which could give away his position, he set it near him at the base of the tree, figuring he could retrieve it in the morning.

Then he settled back to wait, concentrating on the jungle around him. The noises that he had heard earlier had faded. Even the buzz of the insects was gone, and it was as if he had become lost in the world of the dead. Glancing upward through a break in the thick jungle canopy, he could see a patch of stars. He watched them for a moment and realized that they were slowly fading, the sky brightening around them.

Cavanaugh turned his head and blinked into the darkness. As he stared, he realized that he could make out the shapes of the trees and bushes near him. The branches became more noticeable against the graying of the sky. Rising to his feet, he picked up his canteen and waited with his back to a teak tree.

Suddenly the jungle exploded with a riot of sound. A screeching seemed to vibrate through the tops of the trees, shaking them so that the leaves rattled. Cavanaugh dropped to one knee and glanced upward. Dozens of monkeys were scurrying along the branches, leaping at one another and shrieking, announcing the morning.

He looked at the trail and saw a human shape lying there— a VC soldier killed during the night. His weapon was near his outstretched fingers. Cavanaugh pulled back, away from the tree, moving to the right, looking for his men.

He found Krung crouched over the body of an NVA sergeant whose throat had been slit. A pool of bright, sticky blood had spread out from the dead man's neck. Krung turned and grinned at Cavanaugh.

Farther to the right he found two of the strikers sitting back-to-back, watching the jungle around them. Each had his rifle across his knees and a couple of grenades near his hands. They were waiting for someone to come and get them.

Not far from the two strikers was a third. He was lying on his side, his hands hidden in a bloody mass on his belly. It looked as if he had tried to push his intestines back into his stomach after they had been ripped from him. His head was thrown back, and his mouth was open in a mute scream.

The other three were huddled near a large bush covered with giant pink flowers. Two of the strikers held their rifles and the third clutched a bloodstained machete. Near them were the bodies of three dead VC soldiers. Cavanaugh could only see two weapons.

The men left their positions and joined him. He looked around, seeing the bodies of the enemy soldiers killed during the fight. A hundred meters away a dozen of them still lay on the trail where the first ambush had taken place. Cavanaugh started toward the site when he saw a couple of bloody trails that disappeared into the jungle. He followed one of them for about fifty feet, then stumbled upon a dead enemy soldier, a half-dozen bullet holes in his shoulders. Cavanaugh stooped to pull the AK-47 from the corpse's fingers. Then he hesitated, drew his knife and cut off the man's trigger finger.

Back on the trail his men were moving among the dead, picking up weapons, searching the pockets for anything worth stealing and taking souvenirs. Cavanaugh knew that he should be trying to determine the enemy's unit and searching for documents that might prove useful for Intelligence in Nha Trang, but he just didn't care. Instead, he was trying to figure out a way, some trademark or sign, that would identify this carnage as his handiwork, which the VC would recognize. He knew that some units of the First Cav left the ace of spades on the bodies of the enemies they killed, but Cavanaugh felt that was too conservative.

He saw Krung taking a trophy from the body of a soldier that he had killed. Anytime anyone found a body with the penis missing, he knew that Krung had done it. Cavanaugh looked at the trigger finger he had cut from the enemy soldier and remembered a necklace he had seen when he was a kid. The curator of the museum in Cody, Wyoming, had claimed that it had been made from the fingers of soldiers killed by the Sioux Indians during the plains wars, but Cavanaugh hadn't believed that the shriveled, blackened twigs were human fingers. It was, however, just the thing he had wanted—a way to identify himself.

He saw one of the strikers sawing at the left ear of a dead VC. Cavanaugh leaped at him, shouting, "No! Don't do that. Stop!"

The man jumped back and screamed something in Vietnamese.

"No," Cavanaugh answered. He showed the man the trigger finger. "Take these. Just these." He grinned. "It'll strike terror into the hearts of the VC. Take the trigger fingers."

He watched as the men moved over the field then, carrying out his order. They collected the weapons, stacking them on the trail. As soon as they had finished, Cavanaugh decided, they would take time to eat a quick breakfast, wrap their dead in a poncho liner and head back to the camp. They would be there by late afternoon. He knew that he should make a radio call, but he had already missed so many checks that it no longer mattered. He could cover that when he told the captain about the ambush. That would make everything all right. He nodded as he watched his men. "Just wait till we get back to camp. The captain'll be surprised."

8

OUTSIDE SPECIAL
FORCES CAMP A-555

Cavanaugh halted his patrol in the trees along the road that led back into the camp. In front of him he could see the runway, the heat shimmering on the semiliquid black surface of peta-prime. Across the airstrip men were moving among the strands of concertina wire, planting new claymore mines, checking the trip flares and booby traps. A cloud of dust hung in the air above the center of the compound where some kind of construction activity was taking place. Cavanaugh could hear a power saw as it ripped through plywood and the pounding of hammers as the plywood was nailed together.

After a moment's hesitation Cavanaugh stepped from the jungle onto the road. He blinked in the bright sunlight and began walking slowly toward the compound, waiting for someone there to spot him and his patrol. They were some distance from the wires, and it was late in the afternoon, so anyone who saw them wouldn't think they posed a threat. They walked along the road for a few minutes, but the activity in the camp didn't slow.

Before he had the chance to move very far, he saw a jeep heading in their direction, the driver obscured by dust and the glint of sunlight on the windshield. Cavanaugh suspected that it was Gerber. A second later the jeep slid to a halt next to him and Gerber stared him in the face.

"What's the story here, Sean?" asked Gerber.

Cavanaugh held up a hand to halt his patrol. He said, "We found a couple of blood trails leading from the site where we had been hit and followed them for a while. We discovered another trail that looked like it had seen some fairly heavy use and set up along it. Hit the VC last night, killing at least eighteen."

"Casualties on our side?"

"One dead," answered Cavanaugh.

"Why didn't you make commo checks?"

"We were having trouble with the radio, and once I'd set up the ambush, we turned it off so that we wouldn't alert the enemy."

"What kind of radio trouble?" Gerber asked

"Haven't really determined it yet, Captain. Figured we'd find out when we got in."

Gerber rubbed a hand over his jaw and stared at the dirty floorboards of the jeep for a moment. "Okay. Get your people into the camp and then report to my hootch. I'll want a full report on your activities during the last twenty-four hours."

"Yes, sir."

Gerber fought the gear knob for a moment, jerking it back and forth until he shifted into First. "I want to see you as soon as possible." With that he roared past the column, made a U-turn, then sped back in the direction of the camp. As he passed the patrol again, he raised a hand in salute and then was gone in a cloud of choking red dust.

Cavanaugh watched him go, grinning to himself. Finally he looked over his shoulder at the men standing there with him. The pole holding the dead striker wrapped in the poncho liner was resting on the ground. The others stood watching and waiting, their weapons held by the barrel and supported on a shoulder or with the butt resting on the ground. They were a dirty-looking bunch. Their uniforms were soaked with sweat and stained with blood, and dirt and mud from the jungle.

Cavanaugh shrugged and waved a hand. "Let's move it."

They picked up the body and their equipment and started for the camp. The column crossed the runway and shuffled through the main gate. Cavanaugh stopped them there and told them to take the body to the dispensary, then go to their hootches and clean their weapons and equipment while he reported to Gerber. He issued further instructions for them to grab something to eat, then wash up after which he would check on them.

He left them at the gate, turned toward the redoubt and walked up to Gerber's hootch. Although the door was open, Cavanaugh knocked on the jamb, staring into the room but unable to see Gerber.

"Enter," came a voice from the left.

Cavanaugh stepped in to see Gerber sitting behind the field desk waiting. "You wanted to see me, Captain?"

"Yeah, Sean, I did. I want to know what's going on. I want to know why you were out of contact with the camp for twenty-four hours."

Before answering, Cavanaugh reached down and unbuckled his pistol belt. The ragged sweat stain around his waist was obvious. He leaned his weapon against the wall and then shrugged, adjusting the shoulder straps of his gear.

"Take it off," said Gerber. "You could have dropped your pack in your hootch."

"Yes, sir. But I thought it was important to get over here."

"Have a seat." Gerber reached toward the bottle of Beam's that was stored in the lower desk drawer, then hesitated, as if thinking about it. He straightened and then said, "Now, then. What happened?"

"Well, sir," started Cavanaugh, "I took the patrol right to the ambush spot so that they could claim the bodies. A couple of us circled the outside perimeter, and I found what I thought was a blood trail. I reported it to Lieutenant Duc and suggested that I take a couple of men and follow it. He agreed. I took six men and Sergeant Krung and we worked our way through the jungle, looking for the wounded soldier.''

"Did you find him?''

"No, sir. We did, however, cross a trail that looked like it had been heavily used, so I decided to set up an ambush.''

"But felt that you didn't have to coordinate that with either Lieutenant Duc or with us here,'' Gerber cut in.

"I tried, sir, but the radio wasn't working properly. It was late, and I figured that Lieutenant Duc would have taken the men back to the camp.''

"He did, leaving a truck and two men behind. Fortunately, he got away with that because the truck returned this morning,'' said Gerber.

"Yes, sir. Well, we tried to make radio contact but failed. I figured that since we were set, we might as well remain in place.''

"Not thinking about us here,'' said Gerber. "Didn't you think that we would be wondering what happened and might field a search party?''

"I did think of that, Captain,'' said Cavanaugh, "but figured that you'd wait until morning since we hadn't indicated any problems. That you'd figure it was a radio problem.''

"Sean,'' snapped Gerber, "that is bullshit, and you know it. You know better than running these renegade operations. When you discovered the radio problem, you should have pulled out.''

"But, sir,'' protested Cavanaugh, "when we learned the radio was out, we were already set and it was nearly dusk.''

"Go on.''

Cavanaugh described the ambush and then the grenade duel. He explained to Gerber how he had checked the radio the following morning and couldn't find anything obviously wrong with it, but that he couldn't contact the camp.

"More bullshit, Sean," said Gerber. "You're the fucking junior commo man. If a radio isn't shot full of holes, you're supposed to be able to fix it."

"But I didn't have any tools for that, Captain. I didn't take anything because I didn't know that we were going to split up the way we did."

"All right, let's forget that for the moment. It's not that important, anyway. The real issue is the way you handled yourself in the field. I don't think you were using good judgment—out of contact with the camp and you went ahead with the ambush, anyway. If you'd run into something that you couldn't have handled, we'd have been picking up your bodies, if we knew where the hell to look."

"But, sir—"

"Shut up and listen, Sean. I don't like this solo shit. I don't like my men running off on their own. This whole thing, from the moment you left the main body of the patrol, was not thought out."

"What's the problem, Captain?" asked Cavanaugh, grinning. "We got away with it."

"Dammit! That's not the point. The point is your running around in the jungle on your own. There is no way for us to lend support if you don't have a radio and we don't know where you are. Fetterman found the ambush point because we knew where Novak was taking his patrol. With you we only knew that you had been in the jungle east of that point."

"But you hadn't sent anyone out to find us," said Cavanaugh.

"That's where you're wrong again. Fetterman was out with a platoon, and I diverted Tyme into the area to look for you. I've called them off now because you showed up, but they were out looking."

Cavanaugh let his eyes drop to the floor. "Yes, sir. Sorry. I thought I was doing the right thing."

"Well," Gerber said, "you're right about one thing. You did get away with it. Now how are we going to prove the body count? Saigon will want some kind of proof."

"We brought in some of the weapons," said Cavanaugh. "There were too many to carry, so we destroyed most of them, but we do have some weapons."

"How many?"

"Just seven of the AKs. Fairly new ones."

Now Gerber smiled. He shifted through the papers on his desk and said, "MACV just came up with a new guideline. Claims that Charlie doesn't have all that many weapons and lets us count three bodies for every captured weapon. Makes your body count twenty-one if we use that."

"There is something else, sir."

"What's that?"

"Well, I really don't know how to tell you, but the strikers took trophies."

"What kind?"

"Krung was taking his normal ones, you know the dead guys' dicks. I caught a couple of the others starting to take ears."

"And you didn't stop them?"

"Well, I'm really only an advisor, and if the Vietnamese want to cut up the bodies, I can't really order them not to. Well, I can, but they don't have to listen—"

"Sean, you're bullshitting me again."

"I told them to take only the trigger fingers."

"You what? Are you aware, Sergeant, of the MACV directives on atrocities? You can't tell them to take the trigger fingers."

"I was trying to keep them from mutilating the bodies and figured that it was the lesser of the two evils."

"Sean, I'm required by regulations to report this to Saigon. They're quite serious about mutilating the dead and taking trophies. We can't condone it."

Cavanaugh felt the blood drain from his face and his stomach turn over. Suddenly he felt as though he was back in the jungle, grenades exploding all around him. He was scared now, afraid that they were going to take him out of the field. Send him to Saigon to court-martial him for cutting the trigger finger off a dead enemy soldier.

"But, sir—"

"No buts. It just can't be done."

"But the Vietnamese did it. I didn't."

Gerber stood up and walked around the metal chair. He stopped facing the wall, looking through the heavy screen at the redoubt. He turned and said, "Listen, Sean, I'm required to report this." He saw that Cavanaugh was going to protest again and held up a hand. "Let me finish. What I want to say is that we can't always follow all the directives written by the chairborne commandos running around Saigon. I should give you an Article Fifteen for this, dock you some pay and give you extra duty, but I'm not going to."

"Thank you, Captain," said Cavanaugh, the relief obvious in his voice.

"I'm going to be watching you, though, Sean. We're short-handed and we need every man, but you can't go running off into the field without coordinating it with me, and you can't tell the strikers to take trigger fingers, no matter what the reason."

"Yes, sir."

Gerber moved to the front of the desk. "You've done some spectacular things here. Pulling three men out of the burning team house, surviving that ambush. But you have to use your head all the time. You have to think things through to see how they may affect others. Now grab your equipment and get out of here. I'll see you later."

Cavanaugh stood. "Yes, sir. Thank you, sir." He turned to pick up his equipment and rifle and left.

Gerber watched his retreating back for a moment and then returned to his desk. He fumbled through the papers on it and read the directive from MACV again. For every weapon captured, it required them to count three enemy soldiers out of action. Since Cavanaugh had brought in seven weapons, he could report twenty-one killed, although they knew the total should only be eighteen. He laughed, wadded up the paper and tossed it at the corner of his hootch. He would ignore it.

He reached down and got out the bottle of Beam's, uncorked it and took a deep drink. He held it for a moment, took a second pull, then replaced the bottle. He was tempted to go out to see how the new team house was progressing but decided against it. Instead, he picked up an after action report that had come with the morning's mail. It had been designed to alert the Special Forces A-Detachment commanders about the actions of the CIDG forces assigned to Camp A-102 during the battle of 9 and 10 March.

The report, in the sterile terminology of the Army, told of Captain John D. Blair's fight to hold his camp under heavy NVA assault. At 3:50 a.m., the first mortars of a devastating attack landed. In the following two and a half hours several of the camp's buildings were destroyed and the communications were knocked out. Two of the Special Forces NCOs were killed in the mortar attack.

An NVA probe on the south was repelled, Gerber read, and with the dawn came air strike support for the defenders. A low ceiling made it impossible for the pilots to see their targets, and the men on the ground directed the firing by sound. Several aircraft were hit and crashed, and attempts to land critical supplies by parachute met with limited success. Much of it landed outside the camp, and retrieval parties came under constant, intense fire by the NVA.

At 4:00 a.m. on the tenth, another mortar attack destroyed most of the remaining buildings. An hour later the NVA hit the southern side of the camp with a human wave assault and overran the runway and part of the south wall. The 141st CIDG Company defected en masse. The LLDB commander, along with his team, hid during the battle.

In a three-hour hand-to-hand fight, the Special Forces team and their Nung irregulars were pushed back until they held only the communications bunker and the north wall. The NVA tried to take the bunker but were repulsed by heavy firing. The NVA were organizing two battalions to attack, but two B-57s swooped down, dropping cluster bombs that devastated the formation, ruining the assault.

Two Special Forces NCOs, Sergeant Vic Underwood and Sergeant Vernon Carnahan, organized the remaining Nungs into a counterattacking force to drive to the men barricaded in the commo bunker and the dispensary, but the NVA shattered the assault with machine guns and hand grenades. Both men were wounded, and Captain Blair ordered the aircraft overhead to bomb and strafe the camp. One Skyraider was shot down, crashing on the runway. Another landed behind the first to rescue the downed pilot.

The NVA then began destroying the remaining bunkers with machine-gun fire and hand grenades, and Blair ordered the camp abandoned. The camp defenders formed a line, and Marine helicopters landed at 5:20 p.m. on 10 March. As they touched down, the LLDB commander led a stampede that left the wounded lying in the dirt as the LLDB and the CIDG fought one another to get on the aircraft. The Special Forces men fired into the crowd to break it up while the Nungs continued to fight on the north wall.

Two of the helicopters were shot down as they tried to take off. One of them burst into flames, and the crew died. The jets flying cover were all hit by ground fire. The Special Forces men tried to consolidate the position, and Staff Sergeant James

Taylor was killed. The camp survivors then exfiltrated into the jungle during the night of 10 March. They were spotted by rescue aircraft about noon on the eleventh. Again the CIDG survivors went berserk, fighting each other to escape and, in fact, shooting each other. The combat ended only when a CIDG soldier threw a grenade into the middle of his friends. Throughout the rest of the day, helicopters attempted to pick up the remainder of the camp survivors, and by dark they were all out.

The last page of the report was a recommendation that camp commanders make arrangements to separate themselves from the locals if they were being overrun. The local Vietnamese population couldn't be trusted and was probably riddled with VC and VC sympathizers. The Nung, the Meos and the Tai, ethnic groups who were hated by the Vietnamese, made steady allies and could be trusted. Plans should include them in the evacuation.

There was a last comment about the LLDB at Camp A-102. The Saigon authorities believed that the lack of assistance provided by them and the display of cowardice was the result of their officer failing to lead them. In fact, the report noted that only the LLDB Operations NCO, Sergeant Yang, had distinguished himself during the fight.

Gerber glanced at the last of it, recommendations that had no relevance to him and his situation. Minh, the LLDB commander, had already distinguished himself a number of times. Most of the Vietnamese strikers were drawn from the surrounding countryside and not made up of jailbirds and criminals as had been the members of the CIDG company that defected at Camp A-102. Very little of what was written in the report affected Gerber and his camp, and he wondered why Saigon would issue it without some kind of classification. It was just the sort of thing that the news media didn't need to get their hands on.

He made a note to show it to Minh and Fetterman and then filed and locked it in the drawer of his desk. Once they had seen it, he would destroy it and pretend that it had never come in. He stood, moved to the door and looked at the compound. The new team house would be ready by nightfall. They wouldn't get a hot meal in it, but they could meet there if they wanted to. Maybe it was time he met with the men again. A lot had happened during the last few days, and it might be best if they discussed it. He felt that something was going to happen soon. He didn't know what it was—he just felt that the pot was about to boil, and the pressure would blow the lid off.

9

GERBER'S HOOTCH IN
THE REDOUBT AT CAMP
A-555

Gerber sat behind his field desk, his hands laced behind his head, and stared at Sean Cavanaugh. The younger man was wearing a new set of fatigues so green they almost glowed. Although it was early in the morning, Cavanaugh was already sweating, the perspiration staining his uniform.

"Got a problem, Sean," said Gerber. "Need to send out a patrol to check on a couple of things and don't have anyone left to do it. Tyme's out with Washington, I need Fetterman here and Bocker has picked up some kind of rash and low-grade fever." Gerber smiled. "Personally, I think he's gotten used to sitting in that commo bunker of his and doesn't want to go out."

"I don't mind going out again, Captain," Cavanaugh said. "So far, we haven't had to stay in the field more than one night."

Gerber leaned forward and put his elbows on his desk. He wondered again if it was a good idea to send Cavanaugh out on his own. The man hadn't used good judgment when his radio failed, *if* it had failed. Bocker had been unable to find anything wrong with it, but Gerber knew that the moisture in the air sometimes shorted out a radio, and when it dried the next day, it worked perfectly. Still, he wanted someone out in the vicinity of the village, and Cavanaugh was the only man he had left.

"I'd like an ambush set up in the region of Cai Cai to see if we can catch anything," Gerber said. "This would be for one day and one night, two at the most. I don't like sending you out without a medic, but that can't be helped. You'll be pretty close to the camp so that we can get you assistance quickly if you need it."

"Yes, sir."

Gerber reached into the top drawer of his desk and pulled out a map of the AO. He spun it so that Cavanaugh could see it and began to brief him on the operation. Given the facts that his patrols had run into the VC to the south and west of the camp and the VC had raided the village of Cai Cai, it seemed that a clandestine operation into the region, an ambush patrol, might have some success. Since it was a hit-and-miss proposition, Gerber told the sergeant that there shouldn't be any trouble that Cavanaugh couldn't handle. Maybe it was the type of responsibility that Cavanaugh needed to help him work through his problems. Gerber wanted nothing flashy. He wanted a quiet ambush patrol that would disrupt the enemy and take no casualties itself. A simple, by the book operation.

When he finished, he asked, "Think you can handle it?"

"Yes, sir." Cavanaugh nodded. "It's pretty basic."

"Basic and simple," agreed Gerber.

"When would you like me to move out?"

Gerber glanced at his watch and then said, "You could leave soon after lunch. Ambush sites are scattered all over the place, most of them within fifteen klicks or so. Take three, four hours to get there, give you some time to rest and then slide off into the night about dusk. An easy day, as a matter of fact."

"Who am I going to take?"

"Thought maybe you could get together with Sergeant Hoai and maybe Captain Minh and pull a team from the Vietnamese strikers."

"I'll get that organized." Cavanaugh got to his feet. "Be ready to pull out in a couple of hours."

"I'll meet you at the gate before you leave," said Gerber. He still wasn't convinced that it was a good idea, but he didn't have an alternative.

Once outside Gerber's hootch, Cavanaugh felt like whooping. It was as if God had decided that his plan was right and was taking steps to see that it was put into effect. Cavanaugh couldn't have asked for a better set of circumstances. Only a few team members were still on the camp, so each of them had to take up the extra duty. Since it was only in the commo department that there was backup, Cavanaugh was one of the few men who could be spared. He hurried through the gate of the redoubt and turned toward the Vietnamese quarters.

He found Corporal Tran sitting in the sun, apparently asleep. Tran had lost a sister to the VC in Cai Cai and had been on the last ambush with him. Cavanaugh crouched, shook Tran awake and then pointed into the hootch, indicating that Tran was supposed to assemble the team.

"We begin a new patrol in two hours. Get the men ready, and then meet me at the ammo bunker near the west gate."

Tran put a hand to his eyes to shade them from the sun, blinked and then nodded. Without a word he got to his feet and disappeared into the hootch. Cavanaugh watched him go and then turned to head over to the ammo bunker.

The ammo bunker on the west gate was not the main storage facility. It was a smaller structure, set into the ground and covered over with PSP and several layers of sandbags. The bunker was designed to hold enough ammunition to rearm the men fighting on the west side of the camp in the event of a massive VC assault. It also held all the spare claymore mines because it was closest to the gate. Cavanaugh stepped around the sandbag wall set directly in front of the entrance and descended into the dim, cool interior. Using his flashlight, he located the claymore mines and began setting them out on the floor, which was constructed of thick, rough-cut planks.

A few minutes later Tran and four other strikers arrived. Cavanaugh pointed at the mines and watched as the Vietnamese took two apiece and carried them into the daylight. Cavanaugh grabbed grenades for the M-79s, carrying nearly fifty rounds from the bunker.

Outside, he distributed the ammo to the strikers and then said, "Pack this with your gear. Tran, I want you to draw a PRICK-10 from Sergeant Bocker. I'll meet with you all at the gate in one hour, in full field gear and ready for a two-day patrol."

The men nodded and walked back to their hootches, carrying the claymore mines and the 40 mm grenades. Cavanaugh headed toward his own hootch and, once inside, opened the doors to his metal locker. He took out a set of tiger-striped fatigues and tossed them onto his bunk. Then he sat on the floor, opened the top drawer in the locker and found his bottle. He didn't need a drink but felt he wanted one. Just a short one to take the bad taste from his mouth and light a fire in his stomach—a pick-me-up before a long patrol where he wouldn't have time to think about booze or listening posts or Lieutenant Novak and the deaths of all those strikers.

He closed his eyes and raised the bottle to his lips, letting the liquor set fire to his mouth and throat, swallowing rapidly so that he didn't have time to breathe. He set the bottle on the floor next to his leg and stared at it for a long time. He could almost smell the bourbon in it. Not the smooth stuff that Captain Gerber handed out, not the Beam's Choice but rougher liquor that seemed to sandpaper the throat on the way down. Rougher liquor to give him the edge he needed, get his mind going, his heart started.

He sat there thinking about being in the field with no alcohol. Nothing around except the stink of rice paddies as they baked under the late-afternoon sun, the stink of the water buffalo pens and the open trenches filled with feces. Then he looked at the pistol belt holding his four canteens and wondered why he couldn't carry bourbon in one of them. Oh, he knew of all the MACV and Army directives that prohibited it, but those were designed for the draftees and the clerks, not for the professional soldier who knew his limitations and his way around. Besides, four canteens filled with water seemed excessive. Three would be plenty. The fourth would be the perfect place for his bourbon.

Cavanaugh got to his feet and removed one of the canteens from its pouch and poured the warm water out onto the floor. He watched the water spread, lifting up a film of red dirt that made it look like blood.

Finally he filled the canteen with bourbon. There was a little left in the bottle, so Cavanaugh finished it, figuring that there was no sense in saving one drink. He slipped into his field gear, adjusted the shoulder straps until they were comfortable and buckled his pistol belt. He was about to step into the compound when he realized that the smell of bourbon would be heavy on his breath. He stepped back to his wall locker, took his tube of toothpaste and squeezed some out onto his tongue, working it around in his mouth. Now he would smell like a mint factory, which was better than a brewery. The last thing he wanted to do was inadvertently tell the strikers that it was all right to drink before a patrol. They weren't professional enough to handle that.

Cavanaugh left his hootch carrying his rifle, one of the old M-14s. He liked it better than the M-16 because it was heavier. The M-16 was perfect in the jungle until they got into hand-to-hand fighting. Then it was like being armed with a mop handle. You could hurt someone with it, but it was more likely that you would irritate them. Besides, he wasn't convinced that the smaller slug from the M-16 was all that effective, although Tyme had told him the smaller round was the deadlier of the two.

As he moved to the west gate, he saw that his men were already there, each now wearing tiger-striped fatigues, each with a steel pot rather than the soft boonie hat and each with a large pack holding all the extra ammo and spare equipment that Cavanaugh had requested. Tran had the radio. Krung stood there, dressed and ready to go, too. Krung wouldn't want to pass up an opportunity to kill Vietcong if he could help it.

Cavanaugh moved toward them, nodded at one or two of them and then began checking their backpacks to make sure that they had everything they needed. It wasn't necessary. They had even more than the standard field issue, carrying so much ammunition that it would take a major battle for them to run out.

As he turned to open the gate, Cavanaugh saw Gerber approaching. Cavanaugh stopped and waited, and when Gerber was close, he said, "We're about set to move out."

"Okay, Sean. I just wanted to tell you not to take any unnecessary chances and wish you good luck."

"Thank you, Captain. I'll see you sometime tomorrow afternoon at the latest."

"At the very latest." Gerber shot a glance at the PRC-10 that one of the Vietnamese carried. To Cavanaugh he said, "Remember to make your radio checks, and if you lose contact, you come back in."

"Yes, sir."

"Good luck again, Sean."

"Yes, sir. Thank you." He turned, opened the gate and watched Krung trot down the road, then slow to a walk as he reached the edge of the runway. The rest of the men followed him out with Cavanaugh bringing up the rear. He quickly caught up to Krung and gave him directions across the open rice paddies and empty fields of elephant grass that stretched to the west from the camp. They spread out, five or six meters between them, and walked along the dikes of the paddies, moving slowly, easily, because they had most of the day ahead of them.

At midafternoon they halted for lunch, which took them nearly an hour and a half. They headed out again and approached the remains of Cai Cai near evening. The patrol spread out, swept through and exited on the west side. Cavanaugh stopped at the edge of the village and looked out into the distance. All he could see were open fields of elephant grass, rice paddies and swamps and hills that sloped gently into Cambodia. He could see no point in traveling any farther because the VC and NVA, if they wanted to move into South Vietnam, would have to pass close to where he was.

Under his direction they laid out the claymore mines in a pattern that ranged outward nearly half a klick and would cover the most likely routes of infiltration. They then attached the firing wires and carefully unrolled the cord until they were among the hootches of Cai Cai.

Cavanaugh set up the firing controls in the hootches that dominated the west side of the village, arranging them in a sequence so that he knew in which hootch were the firing controls for which mines. In the hootch farthest to the north were the controls of the mines on the farthest trails; in the hootch farthest to the south were those of the closest. By monitoring movement in the fields with the help of Navy binoculars and a starlight scope, he would be able to ambush the enemy by remote control.

As the sun set, Cavanaugh spread his men out in the village using the decaying hootches as cover. He let the strikers cook their evening meal, using the hootches to conceal the smoke, and then waited. Cavanaugh circulated among them, telling them not to shoot until he passed the word and then to use the grenade launchers. By lobbing the shells, they could conceal the flash of the weapons, and it might confuse the VC. As a last resort, or if the VC attack turned toward them, then they should use their rifles.

When it was dark, Cavanaugh moved to the northern end of the village, worked his way to the west about fifty meters and settled into the corner of a rice paddy where he could watch the fields to the west. He used the binoculars to sweep from the edge of Cai Cai out to near the Cambodian border, looking for movement. He stared through the instrument, concentrating and ignoring the persistent buzz of insects as they swarmed around his head. He ignored the thirst he felt, only occasionally thinking of the bourbon on his hip. He didn't really need it, but the weight of it was a reminder that it was there.

For an hour he watched the fields. The moon came up, bathing the ground in its bright white light and giving the paddies a life of their own. Cavanaugh watched the shadows shifting in the light breeze that did little to cool and thought about his bourbon. Finally, having spotted nothing coming near him, he rolled to his side, tugged at the snaps on his canteen cover and pulled out the bourbon.

The rubber of the canteen retained some of the heat of the day, and as he unscrewed the cap, he was almost overpowered by the smell of the liquor. He held it under his nose for a moment, letting the vapors waft into his nostrils. Then he put the canteen to his lips and took a deep drink. The bourbon felt good going down but tasted terrible. Maybe it was because it had been hot during the day, or maybe it was the rubber of the canteen reacting with the bourbon. Cavanaugh didn't care one way or the other. He sipped his bourbon, thought about it and then took a final deep gulp.

As he put his canteen away, he thought he saw movement in the distance. He put the binoculars to his eyes again and studied the shadows for a moment until they seemed to solidify and take on human form. When he was sure that it wasn't the moonlight, breeze and shadows playing tricks on him, he crawled back to the edge of the village, got to his feet and ran into the first of the hootches. There he grabbed the starlight scope and swept the field with it. In seconds he had confirmed that there were men moving in front of him. Five men spread out slightly but not enough so that he couldn't get them all with one of the claymores.

He tapped one of the strikers on the shoulder and pointed. The man picked up an M-79 and loaded it but didn't fire it. Cavanaugh tracked the VC and then picked up the firing control for the claymores. He watched them closely, excited by the prospect of killing five of the enemy so quickly, so easily. They had been in place for only a couple of hours, and already they were about to score. He grinned to himself and felt excitement twist his stomach. He wanted to take a drink to celebrate the luck but decided to wait until he had made the kill. That was the proper time to celebrate.

Cavanaugh set the claymore control down and dried his sweating palms on the front of his fatigues, watching the five men moving through the night. He wanted to jump and scream but knew that he couldn't. He felt for the claymore controls and picked them up again, his thumb dancing against the firing control, anticipating the action. His eyes were narrowed as if he was staring through a dark tunnel. All he could see were the five men walking along a rice paddy dike a couple of hundred meters away.

He turned to look at his two strikers, then returned his attention to the field. The five enemy soldiers were close to one of the ambush sites. Cavanaugh moved to the wall and leaned forward as if that would help him see better. Then, suddenly, convinced that he had let them walk too far, he fired the first of the mines. There was a flash of light as the C-4 detonated, the explosion quickly following. Four of the men went down immediately, but one of them turned to run. Cavanaugh fired a second mine and watched as the man was blown off his feet.

"You see that?" Cavanaugh demanded, his voice high and strained with excitement, almost too loud. "You see that?" He glanced at the strikers and then peered back into the dark. "Got them all. All five of them."

A sudden burst of machine-gun fire interrupted him. He saw the strikers dive for cover and then saw a stream of green tracers raking the village to the south. There were dull smacks as the slugs hit the hootches. A smaller weapon, probably an AK-47, opened fire, but none of the rounds struck near Cavanaugh's position. Because there was a machine gun firing, he assumed there was a full squad of VC, maybe a platoon of them, that he hadn't seen.

"Tran," he whispered, "use the M-79. Pop a few rounds out there near the muzzle-flashes. High arc."

Tran didn't move immediately, and Cavanaugh reached out to grab the weapon. He snapped the sight down out of the way, aimed the grenade launcher out the window at a high angle but holding it below the sill so that the flash wouldn't be visible. He pulled the trigger and then jumped up to watch for the detonation. The round exploded short of the machine-gun position, throwing up a fountain of sparks and fire.

Cavanaugh increased the angle and fired a second round as more enemy weapons began to shoot into the village. He heard a couple of rounds slam into the mud of the hootch's walls over his head. The VC still didn't know where he hid. They were shooting at the likely locations.

Outside, the round he fired had the distance but was off to the right. He heard a couple of muffled pops as the men in the other hootches fired their grenade launchers. Cavanaugh giggled as he slammed another round into his weapon and aimed it. The firing from the rice paddies and elephant grass increased as more weapons joined in the battle.

Cavanaugh fired, missed and became impatient. He tossed the M-79 back to Tran. "Keep putting out rounds."

Tran took the weapon, moved to the right and then ducked out the door. Using the corner of the hootch for cover, he began shooting as rapidly as he could, using the muzzle-flashes as aiming points.

Cavanaugh crouched at the side of the window, watching the enemy movements. He fingered the claymore controls he held, figuring that he could kill more of them with the claymores than with the M-79. He was just waiting for someone to move so that he could blow them apart with a mine.

He saw a couple of men running across one rice paddy, their heads down as if leaning into a driving rain, heading toward where a couple of the claymores were hidden. Cavanaugh gritted his teeth and mumbled under his breath, "Get them. Get them," because he didn't have the control for those mines. A moment later there was an explosion in the field. Krung or one of the Vietnamese fired a claymore, and the enemy disappeared in the cloud of steel ball bearings from the mine.

That seemed to excite the enemy. Or frighten them. Suddenly there were fifty VC on their feet, running across the open ground. They were shouting, screaming and shooting from the hip, charging into the village. There was a bugle blaring and a machine gun hammering, the rounds pouring into the hootches.

Cavanaugh snatched his rifle, flicked off the safety and aimed at one of the men. He grinned as he pulled the trigger and watched the man tumble to the ground. He sighted on another, fired, missed and fired again.

Around him, from the other hootches, the strikers began shooting, some of them going to full automatic, putting out rounds rapidly, their red tracers bouncing across the fields, and high into the night sky. Those rounds were answered by green-and-white ones from the enemy that raked the village. The sound of firing increased until it was a continuous roar without individual reports. Some of Cavanaugh's strikers used their M-79s, dropping the HE grenades among the men charging at them.

Cavanaugh emptied his weapon, dropped the magazine to the dirt floor of the hootch and clawed at his bandolier, pulling another free. As he slammed it home, three of the VC collapsed as a grenade exploded near them in a mushroom of strobe light and whining shrapnel. Another fell, apparently the result of rifle fire.

Then another of the claymores detonated, taking out half the enemy, the steel balls chopping men off at the knees, or the waist, or the neck. The ground around the survivors seemed to erupt as one of the grenadiers switched to white phosphorus, setting the paddy field on fire. Cavanaugh laughed out loud as he saw the confusion among the enemy soldiers. Some of them had stopped firing or stopped running, and the wailing notes of the bugle faded.

With that the assault broke. The surviving enemy tossed their weapons, some of them throwing their hands in the air, screaming, *"Chieu hoi. Chieu hoi."* Others ran back the way they had come, fleeing toward Cambodia and safety.

Cavanaugh continued to fire, shooting at the retreating men, picking them off one by one, laughing as he watched each fall, cartwheeling into the dirty rice paddy water, stumbling to the ground to lie still or blasted from his feet. From one of the other hootches there was continued rifle fire as a striker did the same. Cavanaugh shot the last of the running men and watched him tumble out of sight in the tall elephant grass just a few meters short of a tree line that promised safety.

Still standing, afraid to move, were seven VC. They held their hands up and continued to shout that they wanted to surrender. For a moment Cavanaugh didn't know what to do. The last thing he needed was prisoners. He looked out the window at them and watched as the men slowly moved toward one another, gathering in a small group as if there was safety in numbers.

There was some shouting from one of the other hootches, the words in a garbled tongue that Cavanaugh couldn't follow. There was a response from the field and another question from the hootch. One of the VC answered, and a second later there was a pop as one of the strikers fired his M-79. The round exploded to the left of the VC. All of them fell, then one started to get to his feet. Cavanaugh shrugged and put a bullet in his head.

For several minutes no one moved. Cavanaugh kept his eyes sweeping over the field, looking for movement, but there was none. He listened carefully but heard nothing. The world around him had taken on the silence of a graveyard. Or maybe it was the silence of a battlefield when the shooting has stopped. Finally he ducked under the window, exited the hootch and checked on the strikers. No one had been hurt, and the closest the VC had come to hitting any of them was when they had put the burst into Cavanaugh's hootch.

He told the men to keep their eyes open, and if they had seen nothing by two in the morning, they could go to half alert. He didn't know whether the VC would try to collect the bodies or if they would stay away, afraid of losing more men. If they hadn't come back by two, he figured they probably wouldn't. Cavanaugh then went back to his own hootch to wait for morning when they could check the dead left on the field, collect the weapons and then celebrate the victory.

10

**VILLAGE OF CAI CAI
NEAR THE CAMBODIAN
BORDER**

The night passed quietly. Cavanaugh spent most of it in the
hootch staring out the window, looking for signs that the VC
were trying to recover the bodies of the dead or that some of
the enemy caught in the ambush were only wounded. But all
he heard were the sounds of the nocturnal animals and insects. Periodically he fingered the canteen that contained the
bourbon as it pressed against his hip, reminding him that it was
there. Once he took it out and shook it, listening to the liquid
slosh around, but then put it away without drinking, con-
gratulating himself on his willpower.

As the sky began to pale, the night sounds outside seemed
to diminish, and Cavanaugh could hear the quiet snoring of
the striker sleeping on the dirt floor across from him. He took
out the canteen, then stood so that he could look out the window. Lumps scattered in the rice paddies and elephant grass
were just becoming visible in the predawn half light. He unscrewed the top of the canteen, held it up in mock salute, then
drank deeply.

A second later he heard a stirring behind him and turned to see the striker sitting up, staring at the rectangle of gray in the window. Cavanaugh slipped his canteen back into its cover. "We'll eat breakfast and then check the field. Count the dead and collect the weapons."

The striker sat there as if stunned and then nodded. He rubbed his face with both hands and then reached behind him for his pack, searching for his canteen.

Cavanaugh watched him and then left his post at the window. He carried his rifle out the door and checked on the men in the other hootches. He found Tran sitting with the radio, listening to the static, the handset clutched in his left hand, although he didn't say a word into it.

Cavanaugh moved close and crouched near Tran. He took the handset from him, put it against his own ear and pressed the button. "Zulu Base, Zulu Base, this is Zulu One Two."

There was a moment of silence and then, "Zulu One Two, this is Base. Go."

"Roger, Base. Be advised that we have made contact and estimate forty Victor Charlie Kilo Indigo Alpha."

"Understand contact. Any friendly casualties?"

"Negative. Will advise when further information obtained."

"Roger One Two. Understand. Zulu Base out."

Cavanaugh gave the handset back to Tran and then left that hootch. He found Krung sitting outside the last one, his knife in hand, slowly stroking the blade against a whetstone. Cavanaugh grinned at him. "How are you going to know which ones you killed?"

Krung shrugged. "I killed some. I only take a few trophies. That's fair."

"All right," Cavanaugh said. "We'll move out in about an hour. Have everyone eat some breakfast, and post one man to watch the field. We can't assume that the danger is over just because it's now light.

With that Cavanaugh returned to the hootch he had used and dug out some C-rations from his pack. He threw out the scrambled eggs and ham, eating the peaches and a tin of bread smeared with runny grape jelly. When he finished, he organized the men so that they could clear the field.

They swept out of the village, on line, their weapons held at the ready. Cavanaugh ordered his men to check the bodies carefully to make sure that each VC was dead. In some cases it was easy. The wounds were so massive that no one could have survived them. Stomachs ripped open by shrapnel or bullets. Giant holes blown through chests. The head of one corpse was missing; another had lost both legs. The men of Camp A-555 removed the weapons from the bodies, sometimes prying the AKs or SKSs from between cold fingers, and then stacked the guns on a rice paddy dike.

Cavanaugh found one group that had been hit by the claymore mines. There wasn't all that much left to recognize. The seven hundred and fifty steel balls had turned the men into hamburger, splattering the ground with a spray of red that had turned rusty in the early-morning sun. The weapons the men had carried were broken bits of equipment, ruined by the ball bearings. Cavanaugh kicked at the remains of one man, and as he rolled onto his back, he left a pile of entrails on the ground. Cavanaugh grinned at the gaping hole where the chest had been and said, ''Got you.''

It took them an hour to check the field. Cavanaugh counted forty-four dead men and sixteen blood trails that disappeared into the elephant grass leading back to Cambodia. They had collected forty-seven weapons including a Russian RPD machine gun.

After inspecting the field, Cavanaugh took his Randall combat knife and grabbed the hand of the nearest dead VC. With one swift chop he cut the trigger finger from the hand and held it up for the others to see. Then he nodded at them.

"You get them all. Every trigger finger. But don't do anything else to the bodies."

Spreading over the field again, the Vietnamese cut off the trigger fingers of every dead soldier. The lone exception was Krung. He didn't cut off the fingers but took the genitals. It was a ritual he'd performed a hundred times. He had sworn on the bodies of his dead family that he would kill fifty VC for each of them and kept track by taking the trophies. No one, not even Captain Gerber, had said a word about it.

When they had finished, Cavanaugh summoned the group to the pile of weapons. "I want each of you to take three, and that includes the RPD. We'll destroy the rest of them." He pawed through the captured stock, taking an AK and two SKSs. He knew they made good trading material. Regulations wouldn't allow Americans to take an AK home, but the SKS was a semiautomatic weapon, and it could be taken to the World.

After everyone had been through the weapons, Cavanaugh led them back to the edge of Cai Cai. He turned and faced the pile of stock. He pointed at Tran and said, "One round, WP. Let's see if you can drop it in the center of the weapons."

Tran grinned, broke open the M-79 and loaded the long 40 mm round. He adjusted the sight, aimed, adjusted it again and then fired. The round fell short and to the right but showered the weapons with flaming debris.

"Nice try." Cavanaugh pointed to one of the other strikers and ordered, "You give it a try."

The man loaded his weapon, sighted and pulled the trigger. The round landed in the center of the pile of captured weapons, destroying a number of them on detonation and spreading white phosphorus over the remainder, melting the smaller metallic parts and setting the wood on fire.

"All right!" yelled Cavanaugh. "Excellent shot! Truly excellent." He clapped the man on the back.

The striker laughed. "I did it."

"You sure did," confirmed Cavanaugh. "Okay, let's get out of here. Sergeant Krung, if you'll be good enough to take the point, we'll head back to the camp."

IT WAS THE MIDDLE of the afternoon when they approached the west side of the base. Cavanaugh halted long enough to call Bocker to inform him that they were coming in, but since they had to cross a field that would leave them open to the camp's weapons, Cavanaugh didn't bother to pop smoke. His patrol, because of its size, would pose no threat, and it would be recognized before any damage could be done.

Once they were inside the compound, Cavanaugh halted and turned to face them. He held his rifle up and said, "Weapons check in thirty minutes. I'll expect every rifle, grenade launcher and pistol to be cleaned. Then we'll have a beer. On me. Questions?"

When no one spoke, Cavanaugh said, "Get to it." He watched them head toward their hootches and thought that they looked like winners. They carried themselves erectly and even though they had spent the night in the field, they didn't look tired. Their shoulders weren't slumped. They carried their weapons as if they were still on patrol. They were good men, and he knew that he could rely on each of them.

As they disappeared into their hootches, he turned and headed for the redoubt. Once inside, he thought about reporting immediately to Gerber but then decided that he could drop off his gear and take a short snort. The bourbon wouldn't have the rubberized taste of the booze in his canteen. Upon entering his hootch, he unbuckled his pistol belt and slipped out of his pack, dropping it in the center of his cot. Then, wiping the sweat from his forehead, he opened his wall locker to get out a bottle. He sat experiencing the customary light feeling that one has after carrying a heavy load for a long time. The sensation was that of being able to float to the ceiling.

He took a deep swallow from the bottle, breathed out and took a second. Closing his eyes, he felt the liquor warming his insides, burning his stomach. He could almost feel the fire wash through him, relaxing him, wiping out the memories and the anxieties that had plagued him. He took a third deep drink and corked the bottle, and as he got to his feet, he saw Captain Gerber crossing the compound, moving toward the team house.

Cavanaugh stored the bottle in his wall locker, surprised that nearly a third of it was gone because he had just opened it. He shrugged, figuring that someone else must have taken a drink. Dismissing it, he stepped out into the bright afternoon sun, put a hand up to shade his eyes and called, "Captain Gerber."

Gerber stopped and turned. "Sean. Welcome back."

"You have a moment, sir?"

Gerber turned, stepped several feet closer to Cavanaugh and then gestured toward his hootch. "Let's go into my office, and you can tell me about your mission. Sergeant Bocker said that you reported fifty killed?"

"Yes, sir. That was an estimate. Number of bodies was smaller, but there were a number of blood trails that we didn't follow. And we have quite a few captured weapons."

"Great. Let's step inside, and you can tell me about it." Gerber moved toward his hootch. He stopped outside and gestured at the entrance, allowing the sergeant to precede him.

Cavanaugh stepped up and in and took the metal chair that sat in front of the field desk. Gerber seated himself behind it, laced his fingers together on the surface and said, "Give me the outline of your report. You can write something up later to forward to Saigon."

"Yes, sir." Cavanaugh hesitated and then described the firefight of the night before.

Gerber nodded throughout the report. Then he asked, "None of them tried to surrender?"

"No, sir. When they saw they were going to fail, they just turned and ran."

"And you kept shooting at them?"

"What'd you expect?" Cavanaugh snapped. "They were the enemy, and if they got away, they'd just come back another day to shoot at us."

"I know that, Sergeant. I just asked a simple question."

"Then yes, sir, we kept shooting at them until there were no targets left."

"Were they shooting at you at that point?" Gerber asked.

"I don't see what difference that makes, sir. Our job is to kill the enemy, and I don't see why we have to stop because they happen to be facing away from us. Shit, sir, at least they were soldiers and not innocent civilians like in Cai Cai."

Gerber held up a hand. "Listen, Sean, I'm only trying to get the facts. There are some in Saigon who won't understand shooting men in the back."

"But, sir," Cavanaugh protested. "I don't see what difference it makes if the bullet hole is in the front or the back. They were carrying weapons, and they had been firing them."

"Okay, Sean, forget it. Just don't put it in the report."

"Yes, sir."

"Now did your men take trophies?"

Cavanaugh hesitated, staring at his commanding officer. "Yes sir, some of them did."

"And you did nothing to stop them?"

"Captain, I complied with the MACV directives by not cutting off ears, but I can't control the RFs on this. I can advise them but not order them, especially with Krung out there cutting off dicks."

"Goddamn it, Sean, you were in charge. You could stop them if you really wanted to. That's part of your job."

"Excuse me, Captain, but I thought we were here as advisors, so I advised them not to take trophies. They just didn't listen to me."

"I'm sorry, Sean," said Gerber, "but I just can't accept that. We haven't had a problem like this, with the exception of Krung, and we have winked at that given the circumstances, but we can't let it spread. The last thing we need is to let the press discover that we have strikers mutilating the dead."

"What difference does it make, as long as they're dead, Captain? I've never been able to understand that."

"Then I'll explain it to you. The difference is that civilized soldiers do not mutilate the enemy dead. There are rules of land warfare, and we obey them."

"But that's a load of shit, sir. You fight a war to win it, and if cutting up a couple of dead bodies helps you win, then you do it. The psychological damage to the enemy is tremendous," said Cavanaugh. "It's a real advantage to us."

"Then let me explain it this way. MACV Directive 20-1 states that we will not take trophies, and that's the way it's going to be. No more of this John Wayne shit and lame excuses about the taking of trophies."

"We're awfully shorthanded," said Cavanaugh, smiling. "We going to stop patrolling?"

"After tomorrow we'll be in better shape. Smith and Kepler are due back, and we're getting a new heavy weapons man. That way you won't have to go out without a second American on the patrol."

"But, Captain, I don't mind. I've got a good group to work with. We trust each other."

"That's what I'm afraid of. I'm sorry, Sean, but this solo action has got to stop. Too many strange things have happened too quickly."

"Like what, Captain? All the patrols have been successful."

"Come on, Sean, we're not stupid. You've missed check-in times, you've let the men take trophies and mutilate the bodies and you've taken chances that don't show good judgment."

"But, Captain—"

"Sean, that's it. No more hero crap with your handpicked hatchet teams." Gerber saw that Cavanaugh was going to interrupt and held up a hand to stop him. "Give us some credit, Sean. You've gone out with the same strikers each time. Yes, I notice things like that. You've run up an impressive kill record and have the weapons to back it up, so there is no problem. But I'm not going to let you run loose like this. We're here as advisors, and if we sometimes expand that role, that's the way it is, but it's not a personal vendetta. Once we slip into that, we're no longer soldiers."

"All I'm doing is carrying the war to the enemy."

Gerber slammed his hand against the desktop. "That's bullshit. How many fingers did your assassins bring back this time? No, don't answer that. I only ask you so that you know that we know."

"I don't understand this, Captain," said Cavanaugh, suddenly sweating heavily. "I don't understand at all."

Gerber got to his feet and looked down at the young NCO. "Let's just say that everyone knows what's been happening, and we don't want it to happen anymore. No more missions without a second American. No more of this running off and doing your own thing. No more convenient breakdowns in the radio equipment. I'll let what has happened in the past go because it is in the past, but no more of it."

"Then we stop being soldiers," said Cavanaugh sarcastically.

"Wrong," snapped Gerber. "We stop being rabble and become soldiers—soldiers with a specific mission, and that mission is to train the strikers. To guide them. Not to assassinate the Vietcong."

"I don't understand the difference," said Cavanaugh.

"The difference is we train the Vietnamese to fight their own war. If we must assist, then we assist. But we're not going to take over fighting the war for them because once we do that, then we've lost. If the distinction is too fine for you to grasp, then you are in the wrong place."

"All right, Captain," said Cavanaugh. "I understand. I won't be a problem for you any longer now that I know where we stand."

"Then I'm glad we had this talk. See you tonight at the evening meal." Gerber grinned. "A hot one for a change. We finished rebuilding the team house while you were out."

"Yes, sir. See you then." Cavanaugh walked out of Gerber's hootch.

11

THE HELIPAD AT CAMP A-555

Bocker had warned Gerber that the incoming supply chopper contained both Kepler and Smith and the new replacement that no one had bothered to identify yet. He was carrying his 201 file with him, along with his orders, and he was a heavy weapons man. He was all that Gerber could ask for.

Gerber had heard the helicopter, the blades popping and the engine roaring, but he hadn't spotted it yet. Fetterman strolled out the gate, turned and looked to the east. The sun was trying to break through the clouds that had blown over the camp about an hour after sunup. He stepped closer to Gerber.

"New man?" Fetterman asked.

"On the chopper," said Gerber without looking at him. "And Kepler and Smith. Bocker confirmed they're on board."

"That's good," said Fetterman, still facing east, a hand over his eyes to shade them from the morning sun. "Especially with Cavanaugh getting weird on us."

Gerber turned to stare at Fetterman. "Cavanaugh's getting weird?"

"You know what I mean. Recruiting that hunter-killer team of his and those ambush patrols. Just a little flaky. Not exactly by the book."

"We do a lot of things that aren't by the book, Master Sergeant. You have a problem with Cavanaugh that I don't know about?"

"No, sir," said Fetterman. "Sure don't. Just glad we've got a couple of the team coming back so that we can put two Americans on each patrol. Help each other out."

Gerber saw the helicopter appear in the distance, looking like a big insect. He said, "If you have something on your mind, Tony, I want to know what it is."

"Nothing, sir. Just commenting on the situation that seems to have resolved itself."

"Then I'll pretend you didn't say anything. It's your job to keep track of those kinds of problems so I don't have to worry about them."

"Yes, sir," said Fetterman, nodding. "I'm keeping an eye on the situation. By the way, when is Miss Morrow due back?"

"Miss Morrow is currently running around in I Corps, interviewing the survivors of Camp A-102. Say, did you know they put the Air Force jock in for the Medal of Honor for plucking his friend off the runway?"

"Didn't know that," said Fetterman. "How about our boys?"

"Haven't heard anything official, but I assume they've gone in for a bunch of stuff. Just not the CMH."

"Well, that figures." Fetterman looked up at the helicopter and grabbed a smoke grenade from his pocket. He pulled the pin and tossed it to the center of the pad where it began billowing red smoke that blew back at them. They stepped to the rear out of the way.

"So," said Fetterman, "you didn't tell me when Robin is going to rejoin us."

"Not really sure." Gerber shrugged. "I imagine that once she gets her story up north, she'll make a pass back by here."

The helicopter had gotten closer, the roar of the engines beginning to wipe out any sound. Both men ducked and raised a hand to their heads to hold their berets in place. Gerber turned his head toward the camp, his eyes closed for protection against the swirling dust and debris kicked up by the blades as the helicopter hovered closer. The noise from the turbine overwhelmed them. A moment later the aircraft settled to the pad, and the whine of the engine decreased as the pilot rolled off the throttle. Gerber looked toward it and saw Kepler leap from the cargo compartment and then reach in to grab his bag. He helped Smith to the ground, and together they began throwing boxes and wooden crates onto the pad.

Behind them a tall, thin man tossed a duffel bag to the ground. He climbed out, reached back for a suitcase and a briefcase. He had one of the new M-16s slung over his shoulder and wore a complete set of combat gear that included a harness, backpack, canteen and a large knife taped upside down to the shoulder straps.

Gerber felt there was something vaguely familiar about the man. He had dark hair that was sweat damp. His face was white, suggesting that he hadn't spent much time in the sun lately. He had dark brown eyes, a long nose and thin lips. He had a solid build. The more he studied the newcomer, the more Gerber couldn't help thinking that he had seen the man somewhere before.

He started to move toward the new arrival, but the helicopter pilot revved up his engine again, lifted to a hover, blowing everything that was light and not fastened down from the helipad, and then rotated the aircraft, taking off the way he had come.

As the helicopter disappeared in the distance, the new man snapped to attention in front of Gerber and reported,

"Specialist Fifth Class William Henry Schattschneider reporting as ordered, sir."

Gerber returned the salute self-consciously. "We normally don't..." He stopped, looked at the man's name tag and asked, "You related to a Master Sergeant Schattschneider who was once my team sergeant?"

"My dad, sir. When he was killed, I wanted to enlist but finished high school and then got into the Army. I volunteered for the Special Forces and then Vietnam and then for this camp."

"Christ!" Gerber wasn't sure exactly what he should do. Or even say. He remembered the letter he had written to the senior Schattschneider's wife and family, and the last thing he expected was that the son would show up. He wondered about Army regulations regarding the sole surviving heir but figured that someone up the line would have checked on that. He realized that he was standing there much too long and reached for the other man's hand to shake it. "Welcome aboard. You need help with your gear?"

"No, sir. I can manage."

"Okay." Gerber turned to Fetterman. "Sergeant, why don't you take Specialist Schattschneider with you and find him a bunk and then take him to the team house." He looked at the new man and added, "I'll meet with you there, and you can let me see your 201 file."

"Yes, sir."

As Fetterman and Schattschneider made their way up to the camp, Gerber moved closer to Kepler and looked at the pile of equipment and boxes that had been left. "You been doing some horse-trading, Derek?"

"Found a few things I thought we could use, Captain," said Kepler. "Most of it was just lying around, so I volunteered it to assist us." Kepler smiled.

"I'll get you some help," Gerber said. "Anything in that mess I should know about?"

"No, sir. Just routine equipment, including a small generator for the dispensary so that we can take that off the camp circuits. It's big enough to run a couple of small air conditioners."

"Well, maybe on your next trip you can find the air conditioners."

"Oh, no, sir," said Kepler, "you misunderstand. I brought those, too."

Gerber couldn't help himself. He burst out laughing. "Christ, Derek. You're going to get us all nailed."

"Don't worry, the Air Force will never miss them."

"All right, I'll go get a truck to haul this stuff into the camp." He walked back up the short road that led to the main gate, stopped and looked back. Kepler and Smith were organizing the equipment so that it would be easier to load.

In front of him, near the redoubt, Gerber could see Fetterman and Bocker talking to the new man. The captain shook his head in disbelief. Schattschneider's kid here. Now how in the hell was he supposed to react to that? Schattschneider, the master sergeant, had been a damned fine soldier who had died, it might be said, dodging the wrong way. Not a great heroic death defending the camp from the yellow horde battering down the gate, but a small quiet death with a piece of shrapnel cutting the life from his body. If he had been standing six inches to the side, he would have had one hell of a war story. All he got was a pine box, a Purple Heart and a quick trip to Arlington.

Gerber tore his eyes away from the scene. Schattschneider bore a striking resemblance to his old man, and in the bright morning sun it was hard to believe that it was the kid. Gerber had greatly respected the old man, had leaned on him when they formed the team. It was going to be difficult to deal with the kid. To be fair to him. Give him a chance to grow, to learn, and not just protect him.

He moved toward the motor pool, climbed into the cab of a three-quarter ton and started the engine. He fought the gearshift for a moment, then roared out the gate in a cloud of dust and diesel smoke.

He pulled up next to the equipment and sat in the cab staring to the west while Smith and Kepler loaded the rear. Across the open fields of elephant grass and rice paddies were the hills that marked Cambodia. At that moment Gerber wondered just what the fuck he was doing. Sometimes it seemed so worthless. Memories of dead friends haunted him. Hell, he had the living reminders of his dead friends in the form of their children haunting him. And there was Cavanaugh. A young man who seemed to have become completely warped by the horror of close combat. Tyme had been correct when he said there were a lot of little things that didn't seem right.

A quick double knock on the side of the truck broke his train of thought, and Gerber glanced in the rearview mirrors. The equipment had been loaded, and Smith and Kepler were in the back waiting. He started the engine, shifted into Low and turned up the road. He drove through the gate, wove his way up to the entrance of the redoubt and stopped. As Kepler and Smith jumped to the ground, Gerber got out of the cab and walked around the back to help the men unload it.

Just as they were finishing, Fetterman approached alone. He glanced at Kepler and Smith and then said, "Captain, we've got another problem."

"Well, that's great," said Gerber. "I was running out of things to worry about. What is it now?"

"I can't be sure yet, but I think Sean has gone over the hill."

"Over the hill?" Gerber snapped. "What the fuck do you mean by that?"

"I mean simply that it looks like he's taken off. I talked to Minh and his team sergeant, and it seems there are a number of strikers missing, too."

"Christ," said Gerber tiredly. "How many?"

"Minh's getting a muster right now. Said he thought it was about twenty-five. Most of them are the guys Cavanaugh was out with in the last couple of days."

"What about Krung?" Gerber asked. "He still here?"

"Yes, sir. I talked to him briefly. Claimed he didn't know a thing about it."

"Right," said Gerber, shaking his head. "Didn't know a thing. Okay. You checked the equipment yet? See what he took?"

"No, sir. Thought I'd better brief you."

"When'd all this happen?" asked Gerber.

"Nobody saw anything. I would guess they left last night sometime."

"Okay, Tony," said Gerber, "let's you and me head over to the arms locker and see what's missing. We'd better swing by supply and see what's gone from there, too. Have Washington run an inventory on his medical supplies."

"Yes, sir. Then what?"

"I guess we'd better get a patrol together, then go out to find the silly son of a bitch, that's what."

IT HAD BEEN relatively simple for Cavanaugh to get out of the camp, even with twenty-two men and all the equipment they could carry. They had decided to wait until three in the morning, when only a few strikers on the bunker line were alert. The only other American who had been awake was on the north wall, watching the distant flares of artillery as one of the fire support bases rained 105 mm shells on a suspected enemy location. The Vietnamese who had seen them had assumed that it was just a routine patrol, and since that was rarely cleared with them, they let it go. If Minh or his LLDB NCOIC had seen them, it would have taken some fast talking to get out, but neither Minh nor the NCO saw them, so the problem didn't arise.

Cavanaugh had taken them out under cover of darkness, then moved them rapidly through the elephant grass and rice paddies until they had come to a tree line. They had entered it and taken up defensive positions to wait for the sun. Cavanaugh figured that it would be a couple of hours before anyone reported him missing, and another couple before a search party could be organized. By waiting for light, he could make better time. If he forced it in the dark, there was a real chance that someone would get hurt or that they would stumble into a VC ambush.

As the sun came up, Cavanaugh moved among his men, checking their equipment. Some of them were loaded down with C-rations, carrying only a little ammo for a single weapon. Others bore spare ammo for the machine guns, the grenade launchers and the recoilless rifle. And still others carried a couple of rifles and a dozen bandoliers filled with extra magazines. There were enough food and weapons to give him time to build a small base camp.

When he was satisfied with all that he saw, he got them on the move. They swept out of the trees, along the bank of a canal, heading straight for Cambodia. Cavanaugh figured that the best place to put his camp was on the other side of the border. It would keep the Americans away from him because they didn't dare cross into a foreign country. And it protected him from the VC and NVA because they knew that the Americans couldn't operate on that side of the line. It was the last place anyone would look.

With the trees and several klicks separating them from the camp, Cavanaugh moved from the soft, muddy ground along the bank of the canal to the broken pavement of a road that had been allowed to disintegrate. They made good time, forgetting about breakfast and ignoring the growing heat as the sun climbed higher. Cavanaugh checked his map repeatedly, used his compass and, when he was sure that they had crossed into Cambodia, began searching for a place for his camp.

The jungle, a thin, lightly wooded area that reached to the bank of the canal and bisected the road, provided cover. Cavanaugh waved his men into it, and moved along the major axis until he found an outcrop of rock that climbed twenty or thirty feet above the surrounding countryside. The trees, mostly palm and teak, and a light scrub of bushes and a covering of elephant grass combined to conceal the rock. Not far away was a slowly moving stream of clear water and near that were several small ponds, a couple of them resembling bomb craters.

Cavanaugh pointed at the rock and told the point man, "This is it. This will mark our first camp."

GERBER STOOD IN THE ARMS LOCKER, a Coleman lantern blazing on the floor beside his foot, and looked at the empty spaces where M-60 machine guns, M-14 and M-16 rifles, M-79 grenade launchers and even a 90 mm recoilless rifle had been. The interior of the bunker was cool. There was a mess in one corner where someone, probably the Vietnamese under der Cavanaugh's direction, had opened ammo crates, throwing away the packings that added weight to the ammo. He stood there for a moment, wishing that he had kept better track of the equipment in the arms locker and then wondered why. He knew that a lot of equipment was missing—he could make an accurate guess at the numbers—and decided that a precise count didn't matter. The weapons were gone, and he knew where they went.

He reached down for his lantern and walked outside. He saw Fetterman coming toward him, carrying a clipboard. Fetterman, who was reading something clipped to it, stopped, looked up and then moved closer.

"Got a list here, Captain. Looks like he grabbed a bunch of C-rations but went through the boxes, throwing out everything that he didn't like." Fetterman grinned. "Tossed out the ham and lima beans, the scrambled eggs, the bread and the like. Kept the pound cake, the fruit, beans and franks. All the good stuff.''

Gerber shook his head. "For a spur-of-the-moment operation, this was well thought out.''

"Yes, sir.''

"Okay, I guess we can assume that he doesn't plan to come back soon. Let's go get him. Find . . .'' Gerber stopped and stared at the ground. "Find Krung and a group of Bao's strikers. No, that's no good. Makes it the Tai against the Vietnamese. We'll take Krung as a tracker, but I'll talk to Minh and get a squad of Vietnamese. Be ready to go in half an hour.''

Fetterman nodded and headed in the direction of the redoubt. Gerber walked toward the hootch that Minh used for his headquarters in the Vietnamese section of the camp. He stepped into the office. The LLDB sergeant waved him through. Gerber knocked on the door and entered Minh's inner sanctum.

Minh had taken over command of the LLDB after Captain Trang was killed during a ground attack. Minh, unlike most of his contemporaries, had been trained in England and spoke English with a British accent. He was slightly bigger than the average Vietnamese, about five foot seven, and had the typical jet-black hair and dark complexion.

When he heard Gerber, he looked up. "Don't see you here often, old boy. What can I do for you?''

Gerber sat in the old settee along one wall and stared at the screen above the plywood wall. "I've got to take a patrol out and would like a squad of your best strikers.''

"No problem, old boy. You've got them.'' For a moment Minh sat there, seeming to study a paper on his desk. "I assume that this has to do with your Sergeant Cavanaugh and my missing men.''

"Yes,'' Gerber said, not exactly sure what he should tell Minh. He trusted Minh, but this was a new problem, something they hadn't faced in the past. Finally he said, "I think it best if I take a team out to find him. Talk him into return-ing."

"That would be best," Minh agreed. "I'll go with you."

Gerber got to his feet. "Thanks, but one of us has to stay here. Since it's my man who's gone bad, I'll go get him."

Minh nodded. "Fine, old boy. Where would you like the strikers to form?"

"Have them meet me by the gate in about an hour. Full field pack and be prepared to stay out for two days."

"Airlift?"

"I think not. I don't want Saigon to get wind of this until I've had a chance to talk to Cavanaugh. Besides, we don't really know where he went, so we're going to have to track him on the ground. Helicopters wouldn't be much use."

Minh got up and walked around his desk to the door. He waited for Gerber to step into the outer office. "I'll get my people organized."

"Thanks." Gerber moved out into the late-morning sun and stared up into the cloud-filled sky. Even with the sun screened, it meant that the hike across relatively flat, open ground would be hot, miserable work. It wasn't something that he wanted to do.

Minh had stopped behind him, looked at the sky, too, and then wandered off. Gerber watched his counterpart disap-pear among the buildings and then moved off toward the re-doubt. Two days and it would be over. He hoped.

12

ACROSS THE CAMBODIAN BORDER, SOUTH OF THE PARROT'S BEAK

Cavanaugh supervised the construction of his camp. He wanted to make certain that the place could be used as a rally point and supply depot, not something that would become so comfortable that it would be hard to convince the strikers they needed to patrol.

He helped the strikers set up claymore mines to protect the perimeter. The outcrop of rock, hidden in the jungle, was ringed with the mines, some of them braced against the rock face; a double ring lined the gentle slope on the western side of the rock. Others were hidden at the base of trees, concealed in bushes and even wired to the branches of teak trees, angled downward to rake the game trail that skirted the edge of the outcrop.

On the top he had the strikers emplace their machine guns and recoilless rifle so that they could command the approaches. And when that was finished, they spread the spare equipment out, burying, hiding and stacking some of it out of the way. When he thought they were ready, Cavanaugh stood at the point of the outcrop and slowly turned. He could see the tops of some trees and bushes, others towered over him. To the east, he caught glimpses of the rice paddies and farmers' hootches there. To the south, west and north, he could see nothing other than jungle, which thinned into swamps and open fields. Thirty feet below him was a small clear area and then a rock face filled with cracks and crevices that led up to the point. A hundred meters beyond that clearing was a small stream that would provide a handy source of water.

He didn't want anything that would be easily visible from the surrounding countryside, although he did let the men construct lean-tos of jungle vines, palm leaves and thin branches. Such structures were common throughout the area, so any VC or NVA stumbling on them wouldn't be overly concerned. They might knock the shelters down, but they might not search carefully.

Cavanaugh sat on the rock, staying in the shadows and out of the patches of bright sunlight bleeding through the canopy and thought about that. VC stumbling onto his camp. The last thing he wanted to do was supply the enemy. He got to his feet, sought out Corporal Tran and told him that they were going to booby-trap their equipment just in case.

GERBER STOOD AT THE WEST GATE, binoculars to his eyes as he scanned the fields in front of him. There were so many paths crisscrossing the ash-covered ground made by the patrols he had sent out that he couldn't positively identify one that might have been made by Cavanaugh and his men. Not that it mattered because once they had crossed the killing ground, he was sure that the terrain would conceal Cavanaugh's trail.

"Ready when you are, Captain," said Fetterman, who had come up behind him.

Gerber lowered his binoculars and stuffed them into the case at his hip. "Where's Krung?"

Fetterman pointed, and the two of them moved over to talk to the sergeant. Gerber asked, "You have any idea where Sergeant Cavanaugh might have gone?"

For a moment Krung stared at the ground near his feet. Finally he looked up. "I not kill Sergeant Sean. He good man. He kill VC. I help you find, but I not kill."

Gerber nodded gravely. "We're not going to kill him. We're going out to bring him back here."

"Why?" Krung asked.

"Why?" Gerber repeated. "A damned interesting question. Let's just say because he's not playing by the rules. We can't let him fight the war on his own."

"Why?" asked Krung again. "He kills VC."

Gerber looked at the Tai and shook his head. There was no way he could explain it. To Krung, the whole point of the war was to kill the VC. To Gerber, it was to train the South Vietnamese to kill the VC. A subtle difference.

It was also a question of discipline. He couldn't have one of his men decide to go out to fight on his own. There were other considerations, many of which he didn't know. Treaties with foreign countries, pressures exerted by those foreign countries, subtle and flimsy agreements that could collapse if a renegade American was running his own war.

But to Krung, Gerber knew, none of that made sense. He only saw the war as a means of killing as many of the enemy as possible. To the Tai, it wasn't a giant geopolitical game played with real men and real countries as the pieces.

Gerber decided to reduce his explanation to the basic fact that every soldier understood, even if he didn't know the reasoning behind it. "Because those are our orders."

Now it was Krung who nodded. "And then what do we do?"

"We bring him home and tell him he has to fight the war by the rules." Gerber didn't like saying that because he believed rules had no place in a war. You either fought it or you didn't.

The last thing you needed was a bunch of rules imposed by a bunch of fat men twelve thousand miles away who didn't understand the nature of combat.

"Getting late, Captain," Fetterman reminded him.

"I'm aware of that, Master Sergeant," said Gerber. He turned his attention back to Krung. "You find his trail. Show us where he went."

Krung stood rooted to the spot for a moment as if he was thinking it over, and then he nodded. He walked out the gate and down the road, across the runway and into the field of ash.

The rest of the patrol strung out behind him, Fetterman taking the slack and Gerber marching near the rear. They crossed the field, stirring up a choking cloud of ash and dust that seemed to follow them, settling on sweat-damp skin, coating everyone and everything.

Once they were across the field, Krung stopped and surveyed the ground. Ranging right and left, he looked for clues but found nothing. He started off along the bank of a canal that reached westward toward Cambodia and discovered the trail. He pointed it out to Gerber, who told him to follow it.

It was near dusk when they approached the Cambodian border. The last thing Gerber wanted to do was cross into a foreign country, especially at night. Instead, he turned his men around, moving a half klick back to the east, and found a good campsite. It was lightly wooded for cover both from the sun and the enemy, there were good fields of fire in all directions and a source of water was nearby.

Fetterman supervised establishing the perimeter, set the schedules for rotating the guards and then prepared his own meal from C-rations. After he had eaten, he made his rounds, checking on the men. About midnight, satisfied with the guard, Fetterman turned in. He had seen Gerber moving among the men, making his own check.

THE QUIET SOUND of distant firing woke Gerber just before dawn. He came awake suddenly and knew exactly where he was and what had awakened him. Over him was the dark green of the partial jungle canopy and under him the soft wet ground of the jungle floor. He rolled to his side, picked up his rifle and moved to the western edge of the perimeter. There he found Fetterman crouched behind one of the strikers who was lying in a shallow foxhole, his rifle propped on a palm log.

"You have any idea what that is?" asked Gerber.

"No, sir."

Gerber listened carefully and then said, "I can hear a couple of M-16s, maybe an M-60, AKs and one or two RPDs."

"Yes, sir," agreed Fetterman. "Couple of grenades went off a few minutes ago, but I couldn't tell whether they were from an M-79 or Chicom."

"That's got to be Cavanaugh's group," said Gerber. "I know we don't have anything out there that could have walked into it, and since it is our AO, anyone else there would have coordinated with us."

Fetterman turned so that he could look at Gerber. "What do you want to do?"

"Let's break camp and move in that direction. I'll want you on the point because we don't want to walk into anything ourselves. You should be able to find them before they see us."

"Yes, sir. How soon?"

"Make it ten minutes. Half the men. The other half will remain here and guard the gear. Take only weapons, ammo and water."

Fetterman moved off into the center of the perimeter and then around it, waking up the men and selecting the patrol. He organized them and ordered them to the edge of the perimeter where Gerber waited, his rifle in hand. Without a word Fetterman crossed into the rice paddies, feeling his way along a dike until they were at the edge of a swampy area, the solid ground covered with short bushes and tall grass. Fetterman skirted the swamp, staying on solid ground but angling toward the sounds of firing.

The shooting was tapering off, but by the sound, Fetterman knew that he was getting closer. He searched the ground in front of him, trying to catch muzzle-flashes, but he saw nothing. The sky was beginning to gray as the sun came up, but the ground was still wrapped in darkness.

Travel wasn't easy because it was still dark, but it was a cool morning with a light breeze. Fetterman kept the pace steady, moving toward the battle but not rapidly. He was looking for the rear guards, or maybe a point, if someone had decided to flee.

Finally they were in the immediate area. The noise of the firing had increased suddenly and then tapered. Fetterman held up a hand and waved the men down, telling them to wait. He crept forward along the side of a rice paddy dike, his feet in the water and mud. He moved his feet carefully, trying to make no noise as the smell from the water in the paddy assaulted his nose. He reached out and touched the top of the dike as he moved toward a line of trees. The shooting, sporadic shots now, was quite close. He even saw a muzzle-flash and turned so that he was moving toward it.

When he was fifty yards away and he could see the trees plainly because of the rising sun, he stopped. He watched the palms and saw a lone man break from cover there, but rather than run, the man jogged along a rice paddy dike. Fetterman could tell from the shape of the weapon and the pith helmet the man wore that he was an NVA soldier.

Fetterman slipped down so that he could brace his elbows on the top of the dike and aimed his rifle, looking over the top of the sights because it was still too dark to use them. He led the jogging man and pulled the trigger once. The man seemed to leap to the right, splashed into the rice paddy and didn't reappear. Fetterman crawled over the dike and in the distance could see the body of the man lying facedown in the shallow water. He watched him for a minute, but the man never moved.

Sure that the enemy soldier was dead, Fetterman moved forward, closer to the tree line. He crawled along a dike, keeping to the side, his left hand sliding in and out of the water. He managed to move within twenty-five or thirty feet of the jungle. Within the stand of trees he could see men running and hear the occasional shot, but he couldn't identify the targets. He watched the firefight, muzzle-flashes that looked like lightning bugs on a hot summer night, and waited for an opportunity to contact Cavanaugh.

While Fetterman waited, Gerber brought the rest of the patrol forward, keeping them as far to the south as possible. He used the cover of the rice paddies and the elephant grass until he could turn north inside a finger of jungle. Gerber moved them as close as he could, then spread them out along the forward edge of the tree line as a blocking force in case the enemy broke in that direction. Through his binoculars he could see Fetterman crouched in the distance.

As Gerber watched, Fetterman inched his way forward and disappeared into the trees. A moment later firing broke out to the right of Gerber's position. He spun, dropped to the ground and crawled toward the shooting. A half dozen of his men were crouching next to trees or lying behind logs, firing their weapons on full automatic, their ruby tracers cutting through the jungle fifteen or twenty feet above the ground. There seemed to be no incoming firing.

"Cease fire!" Gerber yelled. "Cease fire!" He waited a moment as the shooting died away and then worked his way up the skirmish line. Looking through his binoculars, he could see nothing other than a light mist and smoke from the gunpowder drifting through the trees. It was slowly becoming lighter.

"Hey!" came a voice from the enemy's line. "Identify yourself."

Gerber continued to stare. He thought he recognized the voice as Cavanaugh's but didn't want to go shouting his name all over the jungle. Instead, he said, "This is Zulu Six."

"Six," came the excited voice. "Advance."

Gerber looked at the men crouched among the bushes and vegetation and then out toward the voice. To the closest of the strikers he said, "Cover me." He slipped the binoculars into the case. He glanced to his right and left, shrugged and then began to slowly inch his way forward.

Gerber stepped around a tree, looked up and saw Cavanaugh approaching him, his rifle held at the ready. "Good to see you, Captain," said Cavanaugh.

"Sean, what the fuck are you doing?"

"I came out here to fight the war. You wouldn't let me do it at camp, so I built my own."

"You know better than that. Get your men together, and we'll head back to camp. My camp. We'll talk about this there."

"No, Captain. I think not. My men and I have decided to take the war to the enemy. You can help us. Leave all your extra ammo and weapons. We can use those. Food, too. And then get out of here."

Gerber took a step forward, but Cavanaugh swung his rifle around so that it was pointed at Gerber. For a moment Gerber thought Cavanaugh was going to shoot him, but then the sergeant lowered the barrel and grinned sheepishly.

"Sorry, Captain. But I'm never going back. I've seen what the bureaucrats in Saigon and Washington do. How they prolong the fighting with their stupid rules and regulations and corruption. How they refuse to recognize the contributions that we make. Or hand the gains we die for back to the VC. We—" he waved a hand to include the men hiding near him "—have decided that it's time to take the war to the VC and finish it quickly and cleanly. You can help, or you can get out of here. But we are not going back to the old system and the old camp."

"Sean, we can't discuss this here in the jungle. Let's go back to the camp. Work this out to everyone's satisfaction."

"No, sir. You take your men and get out. Leave half your weapons because we can use those. If you don't leave, we'll take them off your bodies. We have you surrounded."

Gerber took off his helmet and wiped the sweat from his forehead. Suddenly it seemed overly hot and sticky in the jungle. "You know me better than that. You have this group surrounded, but this is not my whole force. Besides, have you seen Master Sergeant Fetterman lately?" he asked ominously.

"No. No, I haven't. But that won't do you any good. Shit, sir, I just want to fight the Communists, not you."

"Sean, come back."

"No, sir. Now please withdraw from the field. And don't come back because we'll be forced to shoot first. I won't ask questions. We'll just assume hostile intent."

The last thing Gerber wanted was a firefight. In fact, he knew that he couldn't let one break out. There was no telling what the final outcome would be, although he assumed that Cavanaugh and most of his men would be killed. Fetterman had probably slipped into position to take out Cavanaugh if it became necessary. One thing Gerber knew was that there was no way he was going to talk Cavanaugh into returning to camp. It was a stalemate.

"All right, Sean," said Gerber. "We'll withdraw, but we are leaving no weapons, ammo or food." Gerber turned and called, "Master Sergeant, we move back."

There was no answer, but Gerber didn't expect one. Fetterman would fall back as ordered but not until Gerber and his strikers were in the clear, and he wouldn't give his position away by answering any questions.

"I'm sorry it turned out this way, Captain," said Cavanaugh. "But this is the way it's got to be. Now please leave, and remember, if you come back, I'll have to kill you."

Gerber retreated to where his men were gathered. As he pulled even with them, he said, "Let's fall back the way we came. Nuong, take the point, please."

Nuong got up, looked around and then moved to the south. The others fell into line and started off. Gerber watched them go and then turned back to where Cavanaugh had been. The young Special Forces sergeant had disappeared. Gerber used his binoculars to sweep the jungle but could see neither Cavanaugh nor Fetterman. Finally he put the binoculars away and started off after the strikers. As they broke out of the trees, Gerber saw Fetterman sitting at the edge of a rice paddy, his rifle cradled in his arms, waiting.

"What now, Captain?"

"We return to camp. Straight back to camp," said Gerber.

"We can't leave Sean out here alone. We've got to do something about that."

"That's right, Master Sergeant, but not now. I didn't understand what was going on." As Gerber moved closer to Fetterman, he shouted, "Nuong, stay on the point. Course one one zero degrees. That'll get us back to where the rest of the patrol is waiting."

Nuong nodded, looked at his own compass and moved off. As the patrol strung out, Gerber said to Fetterman. "We'll have to deal with this discreetly, and I don't think a shoot out between us and Cavanaugh is discreet."

"You know, sir, from what I could tell, that ambush of Sean's was beautifully executed. The VC had no chance to counterattack. The few survivors had to flee for their lives. The VC left a lot of equipment in the field for Sean to use. The longer he's out here, the tougher it's going to be to get him."

"But right now," said Gerber, "we've got to get the patrol back to camp. Then we can worry about Cavanaugh. I think we can assume that he can take care of himself for the time being."

"Yes, sir," said Fetterman, grinning. "And I think we can assume that he's getting stronger every day, too. Pretty soon he might just come after us."

"That'll make it easier," said Gerber. "That'll make it much easier."

13

SPECIAL FORCES CAMP
A-555

Lieutenant Colonel Alan Bates sat in the cargo compartment of the UH-1D helicopter and watched the landscape slide by beneath him. For the first time in a couple of months, Bates was happy to be going out to Camp A-555 because he didn't have to investigate the camp commander or one of the other Special Forces men assigned to it.

This time he had good news in the form of a Silver Star for Sean Cavanaugh. Unlike the defense of the listening post nearly a year earlier, this award hadn't been downgraded by the chairborne commandos in Saigon. General Hull, because he was a major general, could approve the impact award, which meant that Bates could deliver the medal and citation within days of the action.

Bates glanced out the windshield of the Huey and saw the star-shaped camp in front of him. As the chopper banked to the right and began to lose altitude, Bates instinctively grabbed for the edge of the troop seat to hang on. Looking down from the cargo door, he saw the camp, the redoubt and the helipad. The aircraft straightened and descended rapidly until it was hovering three feet above the pad, which was made of PSP and lined with rubberized sandbags.

As they settled to the ground, Bates grabbed his dispatch case, overnight bag and rifle. He dropped to the ground and stepped away as the helicopter lifted again, creating a whirlwind of dust and debris that hid the surroundings. The chopper turned and climbed out to the north.

"Colonel Bates," said a voice nearby.

Bates spun and saw Bocker. "Yup, I've arrived."

"Didn't expect you in until a little later," said Bocker, reaching for the overnight bag.

"I've got it," said Bates. Then he added, "Got an earlier flight out and thought I'd spend the afternoon in your team house sipping beer and swapping lies with Gerber."

Bocker led Bates off the helipad, around the redoubt and into the team area. As they walked, he said, "Captain Gerber is out on patrol right now. He's due back in a couple of hours."

"Well, I'll let Fetterman talk to me, then," he said, smiling.

"I'm afraid that Sergeant Fetterman is out, too." Bocker halted near the door to the team house, unsure of what to do or where to put Bates's bag.

"That's a little sloppy," said Bates. "With the trouble you've had out here in the last few weeks, I would expect that one of them would be on the camp at all times."

"Yes, sir," said Bocker. "But this was a short patrol and is coming back this afternoon."

Bates looked at the sun and then at the team house. "Why don't we get out of the heat?" said Bates.

"Oh, of course, sir." Bocker gestured at the door. He followed Bates in and asked, "Would you like something to drink, sir?"

"Give me a beer," said Bates. "Oh, and why don't you have Sergeant Cavanaugh stop by, too. I'd like to talk to him since he's the reason I'm here."

Bocker looked uncomfortable. "I'm afraid Sergeant Cavanaugh is out on patrol."

"Uh-huh," said Bates. "Is there anybody on camp? Other than yourself, that is?"

"Yes, sir. Sully Smith is out working along the bunker line, putting in some claymore mines. Sergeant Tyme is in one of the mortar pits. Sergeant Kepler is with the FNG. Sergeant Washington is in the dispensary."

"You mean Gerber's out without a medic?"

"Sergeant Washington had some people to treat here and the captain didn't think he'd be making contact."

Bates slipped into a chair. "Where's that beer?"

Bocker opened the refrigerator and got out a cool can. He handed it to Bates and then asked, "Is there anything else?"

"Yes, there is." Bates pointed to the other side of the table at an empty chair. "Why don't you sit down and tell me exactly what the hell is going on here?"

"I've really got to get back to the commo bunker, sir," said Bocker. "I've only got my Vietnamese counterpart on duty there."

"I'm sure he's capable of handling anything that comes up," said Bates. "I want to know what is happening out here. There are a couple of things that I just don't understand. Thought maybe you could fill me in on the situation."

"I'm afraid you've confused me, sir," said Bocker.

"Let me lay it out for you," said Bates. "There's something happening on this camp that isn't right. You've lost your executive officer and had a fairly large patrol wiped out. You've had three men wounded—"

"Two of them are back, sir," said Bocker.

"You've had three men wounded," said Bates again. "Your Sergeant Cavanaugh has been involved in each of those. Not to mention where he's just come from. Now I arrive to find Captain Gerber, Sergeant Fetterman and Sergeant Cavanaugh out on a patrol. I don't like it."

"Yes, sir," said Bocker. He stood up and said, "You'll have to talk to the captain about that."

"No, Sergeant, I'll talk to you about it. Now you sit back down and tell me exactly what is happening here. And tell me now."

Bocker stood for a moment staring at Bates. Bocker knew that he was one officer who couldn't be bullshitted. Bates was in tune with the Special Forces and the Army. He knew how the enlisted men thought, how the junior officers thought, and he knew how the colonels and generals, so far removed from the mainstream, thought. While Brigadier General Billy Joe Crinshaw, sitting in his office in Saigon, could be convinced of things that weren't true because he was so out of touch with everything, Bates could not be.

Bocker also knew that Gerber had confided in Bates in the past. He knew that Gerber had told Bates the real details of earlier raids into Cambodia or how needed equipment had been obtained. It was Bates who had helped spring Fetterman and Tyme when Crinshaw had tried them for murder. In fact, Bates had even gone into the field with them more than once.

Slowly Bocker slipped into a chair. He didn't know how much he should, or how much he could, tell Bates. Finally he decided that it was somewhere between the complete truth and an out-and-out lie.

"Sergeant Cavanaugh, ah, went . . . I guess you could say AWOL, and the captain has gone to get him."

"AWOL?" said Bates. "Where did he go AWOL?"

"Out into the field. Out on a patrol. Searching for something. I don't know what."

Bates rubbed his face with his hand, aware that he needed a shave and aware that it was damned hot, even in the team house. The tin roof seemed to be absorbing the heat rather than reflecting it. He took a sip from his beer. "That sounds like a load of crap to me, Sergeant."

"Yes, sir," Bocker replied nervously. "But it's true."

"True it may be, but it sounds like crap, and I suspect there is more to it than that."

Again Bocker stood. "I should get back on duty." He turned and fled as rapidly as possible, expecting to hear Bates yell at him, but that never happened.

IT WAS MIDAFTERNOON when Gerber finally saw the camp shimmering in the heat in the distance. A thin cloud of dust and smoke rose from near the center where construction of a new bunker was taking place. Gerber called a halt and sat down on the rice paddy dike, the heat nearly overwhelming him. He could feel the sweat pouring from his body, soaking his already damp clothes. His mouth felt cottony and his breathing was rapid as though he couldn't get enough air. He put a hand to his eyes and with a great effort looked up at the sun.

This was the worst he had ever felt. It was as if he had sprinted a hundred meters, two hundred, and then, without rest, sprinted again. He wondered if it was because he was getting old, if the climate was beginning to affect him or if it was the nature of his last mission. Maybe a combination of them all.

He shot a glance at Fetterman, who was sitting off to one side, looking as fresh as he did the day before. There were sweat stains on his uniform, as there were on everyone's, but somehow Fetterman looked cooler.

Gerber finally managed to glance at his watch, saw that they had been sitting there for fifteen minutes and forced himself to his feet. Krung, who had been on the point since they had left the campsite, leaped up and trotted into the distance. The patrol, taking its cue from that, got up and began to march again.

When they were about fifteen minutes from the camp, Gerber called in on the radio to alert Bocker.

Bocker acknowledged and then added, "Be advised that Crystal Ball is here. He seeks knowledge about our stray chick."

"Well, shit," said Gerber, looking at the radio. Over the air he said, "Understood. Advise Crystal Ball of our location. Zulu Six out."

He gave the handset back to the RTO and muttered, "That's all we need. A surprise visit from the brass."

At that moment Krung turned and looked back. Gerber raised a fist in the air and pumped it twice, telling Krung to hurry. Krung trotted off, reached the field of burned grass and ran across it. He halted at the runway, waited until the majority of the patrol was close and then ran up the road to the gate.

A few minutes later Gerber, Fetterman and the patrol followed him into the camp. Bates stood there waiting, a beer in each hand. He gave one to Gerber, turned and let Fetterman have the second.

"You boys look like you could use a drink," Bates greeted.

Gerber slipped the can into his pocket. "You don't know the half of it, but you should have brought a case."

Bates nodded. "I understand. My mistake."

Fetterman said, "Let me have your weapon, sir, and I'll see that it gets cleaned." He turned to the men and shouted, "Weapons check in thirty minutes." He held up the can of beer that Bates had handed him and added, "I'll bring the beer."

Gerber studied Bates for a moment and then suggested, "Let's go over to my hootch so we can talk."

"Fine. Lead the way."

As they entered the hootch, Gerber pulled the beer out of his pocket and set it on the tiny field desk. He unbuckled his pistol belt and slipped the harness from his shoulders, dropping the equipment pack to the dirty floor. He picked up the beer, moved around the desk so that he could sit down and opened the bottom drawer. He pulled the bottle of Beam's out.

"You care for a drink of this?"

Bates reached out and took the bottle. He pulled the cork, set that on the edge of the desk and then drank deeply. As he handed the bottle back, he remarked, "That's smooth."

"Yes, sir," said Gerber, reaching for the bottle. He drank, then returned it to the desk drawer. As he opened the beer, he queried, "What can I do for you?"

"Well, for one thing, you can get Sergeant Cavanaugh. I've got an impact Silver Star for him. General Hull signed the paperwork this morning authorizing it, and the reason for its being an impact award is so that we can give it to the man as quickly as possible."

"Yes, sir," said Gerber. He suddenly felt as if an elevator had dropped out from under him. To cover his anxiety, he said, "Sergeant Cavanaugh is on patrol."

Bates glared at him for a moment and then said, "Cut the crap, Mack, I know he's AWOL. You want to tell me about it?"

Gerber rubbed his hand over his face. He leaned forward, his elbow on the desk, his hand over his mouth. "It's a delicate situation. One that we have to be careful with."

"I'm aware of the facts leading up to this point, and you know that the last thing I want to do is nail some guy's ass to the wall, especially one who has been through what Cavanaugh has been through. But there comes a point when we have to draw the line."

"Yes, sir." Gerber picked up his beer and drank. He held the can in both hands, staring at the top of it. "I guess you could say it all started right after we got here. That is, to this camp. It all started with the defense of the listening post and the destruction of the tiny force manning it."

"I'm aware that Sergeant Cavanaugh had some mental problems dealing with that."

"And you probably know that Sergeant Cavanaugh has not reached his twentieth birthday. He is not allowed to vote for the President, he is not allowed to buy liquor, or enter into contractual agreements without a cosigner who can be held responsible. By most standards of our society, he is not an adult. Hell, if he could find a job as a police officer, he wouldn't be allowed to carry a gun until he was twenty-one. This is the man we sent, I sent, out to guard the listening post."

"Yes," responded Bates wearily. "I know all that."

"Then what you don't know is that he was on patrol with Lieutenant Novak when it was wiped out."

"I knew about that," said Bates. "I read the after action report."

"And you know that Cavanaugh was the sole survivor of that, too? Watched everyone with him die in the hand-to-hand fighting, just like the listening post fight."

"Yes, I know."

"Then are you aware that it was Cavanaugh who led the patrol into Cai Cai and found the remains of the villagers after the Vietcong had swept through killing everyone?"

"No, I wasn't aware of that."

"Okay," Gerber said. "Now I know you've seen some pretty raw shit during your career. So have I. But the difference, I think, is the age. Nineteen is just too young to be thrown into a combat environment. Sure, each of us saw some shit when we were younger, but nothing like what Cavanaugh has been through. It took me two wars to see everything he's seen in what works out to only a few weeks in the field."

"You've made your point, Mack. There are extenuating circumstances. You get Cavanaugh back, and I'll have him transferred to my staff. He can finish his tour in Vietnam, and nobody ever has to know about this."

"Yeah, well, there's the problem," said Gerber.

Bates smiled. "You mean there's more?"

"A lot more, I'm afraid. After finding the villagers and the ambush, Cavanaugh organized a team of his own. I guess you could call it a hunter-killer team. Strikers who had lost relatives in Cai Cai. When he went out on patrol, he took these men."

"And you let him do it?"

"Well, sir, it's not quite as cut-and-dried as it appears now. Cavanaugh's idea of an elite team wasn't all that bad. I mean, it gave the strikers some kind of goal. If they were good enough, maybe Cavanaugh would ask them to join. I sort of winked at it because I couldn't see the harm. Then after they had taken the trigger fingers—"

"Hold it right there, Captain," snapped Bates. "Are you telling me that you have knowledge of mutilations of the dead?"

Gerber looked at the floor and took a deep breath. He rubbed his forehead with a finger as if lost in thought. Finally he said, "Yes, sir, I'm afraid I am."

"And you're familiar with MACV Directive 20-4, which governs conduct in the field?"

"Yes, sir. In fact, I briefed Sergeant Cavanaugh on it."

"Mack, you've put me in a real awkward position here. I don't know if I should terminate this interview right now and advise you of your rights under the *Uniform Code of Military Justice*, or just pretend that I've heard nothing."

"In my defense," said Gerber, "let me say that it wasn't my men who committed the mutilations but the Vietnamese strikers. I'll tell you the same thing that Cavanaugh said to me. We're advisors, and we advised them not to cut off the trigger fingers."

"You know that won't hold water."

"Yeah, I told that to Cavanaugh. Anyway, I ordered him to stop it, also any more solo John Wayne shit. I told him the wounded men were returning to camp, we had a replacement coming in and from now on, all patrols would have two Americans on them. That's when he took off."

"Took off?" Bates repeated.

"Yes, sir. Him and about twenty-five strikers—Captain Minh still hasn't gotten a full muster. Went off into the woods to wage their own war."

"Are you sure of this?"

"Oh, yes, sir. I managed to track him down."

"So where is he?" snapped Bates.

"Had to leave him in the field. Couldn't convince him to come back in."

"Christ, Gerber, this is a fucking mess. I saw your patrol come back. You could have forced him."

"No, sir, not without a fight, and the last thing I wanted was to initiate a fight between two elements of the strike force, even if one of those elements was operating illegally."

Bates could stand it no longer. He had to get up and move. He paced across the floor, to the wall, back again and then stopped directly in front of Gerber's desk. "Mack, this is one fucked up mess. I don't understand how you could let things get so far out of hand. You've got a good head on your shoulders, but you let Cavanaugh walk all over you."

"As I said, it wasn't quite as cut-and-dried as it seems now. Sure, I let Cavanaugh have a little more rope than I would any other member of the team, except Fetterman, but given the circumstances, I felt it was necessary."

"Necessary, shit. I'd like to see your medical degree. You should have had Cavanaugh back in Saigon."

Now Gerber was angry. "Fuck that. The man deserved every break I gave him. He earned that much. Now I have a problem to deal with and saying that those pissants in Saigon could do anything about it is ridiculous."

"Captain Gerber!" Bates reprimanded sharply.

"I have a loyalty to the men on the team. We work together, live together and die together, and I'm not about to throw one to the dogs because of—"

"Mack," Bates interjected, "I understand." He held up a hand to stop further protest. "I really do. But we can't have anyone going out on his own. Cavanaugh has to be stopped."

"Yes, sir," Gerber agreed quietly. "I know that. I'll take care of it. Quietly, discreetly, quickly."

"You had better, or else Saigon will have your ass. And mine, too."

"Don't worry, Colonel. It's in the bag." Gerber met Bates's stare. He wasn't sure that anything was in the bag, but he knew that the problem was his to solve.

14

SPECIAL FORCES CAMP
A-555

Gerber stood in the arms locker and studied the weapons that were available to him. In the course of outfitting the camp, he had been given practically every weapon manufactured for the U.S. Army, with the exception of the larger artillery pieces and a tactical nuclear device. He had variations and modifications of those weapons and a few jury-rigged items, such as the flashlight mounted to a rifle stock they had used a couple of months earlier. There were grenade launchers, LAW rockets, a bazooka with a number of 3.5 inch rockets, Fetterman's flamethrower, a mortar and even a Soviet-made RPG-7 with a supply of spare grenades.

He sat on a crate of grenades and stared at the arsenal. In the corner was the one that he needed, but he refused to look at it. He knew it was there, and he knew what it was used for, and once he acknowledged it, he would have to act. By studying all his options, he was ignoring the only one that he had.

Finally his eyes fell on the special M-14, designated an XM-21. It was equipped with a Redfield three-power to nine-power range finder scope. There was also a package that contained a bipod and a sound suppressor, which reduced the velocity of the escaping gases to below that of sound but didn't affect the velocity of the round.

He rose and moved across the rough planking of the floor. In the dim light he stared down at the weapon, which was locked in a rack with a dozen other M-14s. He rubbed the sweat from the palms of his hand, then touched the lens caps over the scope.

"You'll probably need these."

Gerber spun at the sound of the voice. Fetterman stood in the doorway of the bunker, a shadowy shape outlined by the bright sunlight behind him. He held out his hand, and Gerber could see half a dozen M-14 rounds in his palm.

"It's a special round that Tyme and I came up with. We loaded them ourselves, measuring the power. They won't misfire, and they have good long-range ballistics."

"Those what I think they are?" Gerber asked. He moved away from the XM-21 and put a foot up on the grenade case.

Fetterman descended the two steps into the bunker. "Yes, sir," he replied. "Leftovers from when we went after the Chinese guy. They won't let you down."

"Didn't help you much," said Gerber.

"That was because we picked the wrong target, not because the rounds weren't any good."

"Tony, do you realize what we're talking about here?" Gerber kept his eyes on the master sergeant's hand.

"Yes, sir. I know exactly what we're talking about. I came by to offer the tools to do it right and to find out if this is the proper course of action."

Gerber sat down again and stared at the floor for a long time. Suddenly his mind, reluctant to contemplate the business at hand, attached a new importance to everything else around him. He could hear sounds outside, men going about their work. There was a roar of a jet that passed over the camp. A couple of men were shouting at each other in Vietnamese.

Gerber raked a hand through his hair, stared at the palm and then wiped it on the front of his fatigue jacket.

"I don't think there's any other choice," said Gerber.

"We could try to talk him in again," Fetterman suggested.

"I doubt that would do any good. Hell, Tony, I tried it when we found him, but he refused to come in. I don't know what all you heard...."

"Very little, Captain. I was too far out to hear anything useful."

"Well, talking won't bring him in. If talking would have worked, it would have worked when we found him. If he was looking for an excuse to quit and a way to save face, it was provided then. But he wasn't interested in it. He's called the shots on this one."

Fetterman leaned back against the wall of green sandbags. He dropped the special rounds into his pocket and folded his arms across his chest. "There has to be a better way, Captain."

"Don't you think I've tried to come up with it?" snapped Gerber. "Don't you think I've analyzed this from every direction? I studied it at length, and I concluded that something happened to his mind in that last ambush. Watching everyone die around him again did something to him. He's not sane anymore. He lays his own ambushes, plays by his own rules, and he takes trophies now. He's not the same man."

"None of which means we should hunt him down," Fetterman observed quietly.

For nearly a minute Gerber was silent. He stared at the floor between his boots. Without looking up at Fetterman, he said, "The only way to handle this is a clean assassination. If we go out with a force to bring him back, it's going to result in a firefight. Many of the strikers will probably die. Overlooking what such a battle would do to morale, we have to consider the lives of those men. They shouldn't die so that we can take the easy road. A single, well-placed rifle shot ends the problem."

"Then what happens to the strikers who went out with Cavanaugh?"

"When the head is cut off, the snake withers and dies. Without an effective leader they are going to come back here. Maybe as a group, maybe only one or two at a time, but they'll return."

"You sure?" asked Fetterman.

Gerber turned so that he could look up at Fetterman. "No. But it's the only thing that makes sense. Without Cavanaugh they're going to be lost."

Fetterman nodded and moved forward. He began to pick through the equipment stacked in the bunker.

"Just what do you think you're doing, Master Sergeant?"

"Getting the stuff I'll need on patrol."

"What patrol?" asked Gerber.

Fetterman stopped rummaging through the crates and faced Gerber. "Captain, you can't do this alone. You'll need someone to track Cavanaugh. You'll need someone for a spotter, and you'll need another back to help hump all the stuff you'll want to take. I'm in on this one."

"It's not necessary, Tony."

"Don't go telling me what's necessary and what's not. You're going out to take care of the problem. Well, it's my problem, too. Cavanaugh is one of the men on my team, and if he's turned renegade, it's my responsibility to deal with as much as it is yours."

"Tony, you don't have to do this. I'll take Krung and a couple of the strikers with me. We can handle it."

"No, sir," Fetterman said. "This is something that we both have to do. It's not something that one of us should face alone. It's a dirty, rotten job, and I'm not going to duck my responsibility in this."

Gerber moved until he was standing in front of the master sergeant. He held out a hand. "I just wanted to make sure you understood that I would take care of it alone. That you were not required to help.''

''I understood that from the moment I figured out what had to be done. That's why I brought in those special rounds. So that you would know that I was volunteering.''

''Thank you,'' said Gerber warmly. ''I'm not sure I could have done it myself.''

''Captain,'' said Fetterman, ''I'm not sure there isn't anything you can't do, once you set your mind to it.''

He unlocked the rack and took out the sniper rifle. As he snapped the lock back in place, Fetterman moved to the entrance and waited. Gerber hesitated for a few moments, then walked to the doorway. Exchanging looks that spoke of pain and frustration, Gerber stretched out his hand for the rifle.

He nodded to Fetterman, then walked across the compound, stopping first in his hootch to drop off the sniper rifle. Afterward he made his way to the commo bunker. He found Bocker sitting behind the wooden counter in a pool of light from a single lamp, his feet propped up, reading a paperback science fiction novel. There was a Coke by his hand and a gigantic cigar sitting in an ashtray next to the soft drink. The tiny lights on the various radios glowed in the dim light of the bunker.

''Galvin,'' said Gerber, ''I want you to lay on a recon flight for this evening. Single ship to work the fields west of the camp all the way to the Cambodian border. Have them stop by here before they do anything else.''

Bocker dropped his feet to the floor and set his book facedown on the counter to save his place. ''Pretty short notice, sir. And those flyboys don't like to run single-ship missions.''

''If they can get gun support, that's fine with me, but we'll only need them for an hour or so.''

''I'll see what I can do. Are you going to wait?''

''No, I've got a couple of other things to do. When you get an answer and have the mission coordinated, get back to me.''

Bocker turned to the radios and said, "Yes, sir."

Gerber left the commo bunker and returned to his hootch. There he examined the XM-21 again. He popped the lens caps and sighted through the scope. He checked the mounting bolts and decided that if he was going to do it right, he would need to zero the weapon. Fire a couple of practice rounds and adjust the scope for his eyes.

Gerber took the rifle and a magazine loaded with regulation 7.62 mm ammo and walked out into the bright afternoon sun. He crossed the redoubt and stepped through the gate. A group of strikers was working in the wire, restringing part of it, checking the firing controls on some of the claymore mines and replacing trip flares that had been in the field for a month or more.

He spotted Tyme working with one of the strikers. Gerber called to him. "Sergeant Tyme, can I speak to you for a moment?"

Tyme looked up and then back at the claymore. He pointed at something and then stood. He patted the striker on the shoulder and then trotted over to Gerber.

"What can I do for you, Captain?"

"You have any of those targets we use to zero weapons?"

"Yes, sir. In my quarters. I'll get you some." He ran up the road and into the camp.

Gerber watched Tyme disappear from view, then turned to survey the empty fields to the south. About five hundred meters away was a clump of trees that had been used as a rally point in the past. Beyond that was nothing other than swamp and river. He considered using one of the trees to hold the target but decided against it.

Two hundred meters south of the camp were the remains of a dike that had collapsed into a paddy. There was a single palm growing from it. The base of the tree was wide, nearly three feet in diameter, but the tree was no more than seven or eight feet tall.

Tyme returned from the camp. "Captain, I've got the targets."

Gerber turned, reached out and took the package. "Thanks," he said. "You have any tacks or nails?"

"In there," said Tyme. "I thought you'd want something like that."

"Yeah. Thanks." Gerber crossed the runway and walked into the open field of short elephant grass. He walked slowly, finding the heat of the afternoon oppressive. He wiped the sweat from his forehead with the sleeve of his fatigue jacket. When he reached the tree, he crouched and opened the package of targets. Using the tacks supplied by Tyme, he fastened one of the targets to the base of the tree, then walked back to the runway.

He sat on the edge, away from the sticky peta-prime, looped the sling of the weapon around his upper arm and braced his left elbow on his knee. Through the scope he had no trouble seeing the target's black square with the notch cut out. He lowered the weapon, jammed a magazine into the well, worked the bolt to chamber a round.

Again he wrapped the sling around his arm, leaned forward, his left elbow on his knee and set the cross hairs on the notch in the black square. He fired once, thought that he could see the bullet hole in the target, centered the cross hairs again and fired a second round. After he fired the third shot, he set the safety and stood. He walked to the tree and examined the target. The weapon was shooting low and to the left. Gerber adjusted the scope and put up a new target.

He ran through the procedure until he was sure that the weapon would put the bullet where he aimed it. He collected his material and walked back to the camp. As he passed through the gate, he waved a hand at Tyme, who was rounding up his work party.

Again Tyme left them. "Yes, Captain?"

"Justin, Sergeant Fetterman and I are going off the camp for the next forty-eight to seventy-two hours. Minh will be running the show, but I want you to watch over our end of it. Just be around to take care of any problems that arise."

Tyme took off his gloves and stuffed them into the thigh pocket of his jungle fatigues. "Yes, sir," he said. "I just—"

"There is nothing we can do about it now. If Animal hadn't gotten killed, he would have been left here. Now there's something that I have to attend to, and I want to be sure the camp is being supervised."

For a moment Tyme stared at Gerber. It was as if he knew what Gerber had to do. He said nothing. "You can count on me, Captain. I'll take care of anything here. Which radio will you take?"

"I hate to leave all our communications to one of the URC-10s, but I can't hump a PRC-10 through the bush with everything else. We'll be on the team uniform. Normal check-in times."

"Yes, sir."

Gerber turned and headed up the road. Inside the wire, he found Fetterman standing near the gate, one foot up on the wall of sandbags. His weapon was leaning against the wall, and his pack was on the ground near his foot. "We about ready?" asked Fetterman.

Gerber was going to shrug but saw Bocker leave the commo bunker, head to the redoubt and then turn. He angled directly to Gerber and stopped a couple of feet away.

"Got a chopper coming in about thirty minutes. Tacked it on to one of their ash-and-trash missions. Said we could have the chopper for about an hour if we need it that long."

"More than long enough. Thanks, Galvin." Gerber waited for Bocker to move off toward the commo bunker and then said, "Tony, let me grab my pack, and I'll meet you back here."

Before Gerber could move, Fetterman said, "I've talked to Krung about this. Figured he could help us find the trail again. He's familiar with the surroundings."

"Good. I should've thought of that myself."

"He'll be here in a couple of minutes. He did go through his 'I will find but not kill' routine again. I told him that was all we wanted to do. Find Cavanaugh."

There was a distant beat of rotors and the whine of a turbine engine. Bocker came out of the commo bunker again carrying a smoke grenade. He trotted past Gerber and Fetterman out to the end of the runway. He pulled the pin on the grenade and tossed it to the center of the dirt and peta-prime strip.

"I better hurry," said Gerber.

Four minutes later Gerber was back, standing at the gate. The helicopter sat on the end of the runway. The last traces of the green smoke were blowing away to the east, drifting over the rice paddies there. Gerber jogged out the gate, handed his weapon to Fetterman, who had already boarded with Krung, and climbed into the aircraft. He crouched near the pilot's seat, opened his map and set it on the radio control heads on the console.

"There's a pretty good LZ about here," shouted Gerber over the roar of the engine as he pointed to a large clearing marked on his map. "Tree lines are a klick apart, but we'd like you to drop us close to the westernmost one."

The pilot picked up the map and examined it carefully. He handed it back and said, "It's getting pretty close to dusk. I don't like being that close to Cambodia so close to dark."

"There's a problem?" asked Gerber.

"No, sir. We low-level in, flare and you hop out. We should be gone before anyone figures out what we're doing."

Gerber refolded his map and jammed it into his pocket. He moved to the troop seat but had to sit on the edge because of his rucksack. He leaned forward, elbows on knees, and took his rifle back from Fetterman.

At that moment the pilot rolled on the throttle, increasing the engine RPM. The chopper lifted in a small cloud of dust and spun until they were facing due west. The pilot eased the cyclic forward as he pulled in some pitch. They began to slip along about three feet off the ground, picking up speed until they were racing across the surface, then climbing slightly to avoid tree lines and hootches. The aircraft turned to the northwest, angling toward the Cambodian border.

As the pilot checked the terrain, they popped up once to fifteen hundred feet, but then dived to three feet. They altered their course, came to a finger of jungle and climbed so that they were flying just above the trees, the skids only inches from the vegetation.

The crew chief leaned around the transmission and yelled, "We're inbound. Get ready."

Fetterman slid across the deck until he was near the door on the left. He put one hand on the pilot's seat and looked out.

Gerber didn't move. As the sunlight faded, he kept his eyes on the clearing below. It was a large oblong area with a single tree growing in the center. He worked the bolt of his rifle, making sure that a round was chambered, and then slipped on the safety.

Seconds later the aircraft flared, the nose coming up as the pilot used the bottom of the aircraft to help slow him. He jerked in an armload of pitch, creating lift on the rotor blades. He leveled the skids and dropped the chopper to the ground.

As soon as they touched down, Fetterman was out the door. Gerber followed him, diving for cover behind a small bush. Krung leaped clear, and the helicopter popped up. It turned, charging toward the trees, using them as cover. When it was two or three hundred yards away, there was a burst of fire, a single line of green tracers stabbing upward, followed by return fire from the helicopter. A flame three feet long leaped from the barrel of the crew chief's M-60 machine gun, the ruby tracers aimed at the source of the green.

Gerber watched the chopper until it disappeared. He then got to his feet and ran toward the trees, Fetterman and Krung following him. He came to a narrow path, a game trail, and crossed it until he was deep in the jungle. Then he stopped and waited for the other two men.

When they crouched near him, he whispered, "We know Charlie is in the vicinity."

"But they don't know we're here," said Fetterman.

"No, but we have to assume they figure someone is. Otherwise, the chopper wouldn't have been here." Gerber stopped talking and then added, "But then, why shoot at it? Gives them away."

"VC close," reconfirmed Krung. "Very close."

"Krung, take the point. Get us out of here, and find us a place to hole up for the night."

Krung nodded, the gesture nearly lost in the last of the fading sunlight. He pushed a branch out of the way, then eased it back into position so that it wouldn't make any noise.

They worked their way deeper into the jungle, away from the trail, angling away from the VC. Moving slowly, stealthily, it took them almost an hour to advance only a few hundred meters. They ducked under branches, dodged trees and avoided bushes. No one spoke, but the trio stayed close enough to each other so that they could see the shape of the man in front. The jungle wasn't the thick, triple-canopy forest that covered much of the Central Highlands. Starlight and moonlight filtered through it, providing some illumination.

After an hour they were tired, soaked with sweat and breathing heavily, as if they had sprinted a long distance in the oppressive heat of the late afternoon. Krung halted near the base of a giant teak tree. Gerber moved to the right and Fetterman to the left, each man watching the ground in front of him, searching for the enemy.

Gerber slowly, carefully, reached to his side and unsnapped the pouch holding one of his canteens. He drank deeply, the water still cool. He then poured some of the water on the go-to-hell rag around his neck, allowing it to cool him slightly.

After a ten-minute rest they were ready to move again. Gerber finished off the water in the canteen because he didn't want it sloshing around as he moved through the jungle. He slipped the empty canteen back into the pouch and waited as Krung surveyed the ground on the other side of the tree. Then slowly the group stole forward.

It was hard work. Walking through jungle wasn't the easiest way to travel, but they had added the strain of not making any noise. The foot had to be lifted high so that it wouldn't snag on anything and then set carefully on the dead leaves, twigs and debris that littered the jungle floor. First the heel. Then as the weight was shifted, the foot was rotated forward so that the pressure was applied slowly. It provided a chance to back off if there was any indication that a twig would snap or the leaves would crumble.

They didn't want to be heard, which reduced the pace to only a couple of hundred meters an hour, if they were lucky. If it hadn't been for the single line of green tracers marking the location of a VC unit, Gerber would have passed the night inside the tree line and then begun the search in the morning. He remembered that only one weapon had been fired, and that could mean there was only a single VC out there, but he couldn't take a chance. He had to get clear of the area.

At midnight, with the moon high overhead creating a spectrum of shadows that danced in the light breeze, they halted again. They spread out in a triangular formation, each man responsible for watching the ground in front of him. They rested there, sweat pouring from them and soaking their clothes as completely as if they had been standing in a tropical rain shower.

Once in position, none of them moved. They didn't bother with their water, didn't brush at the insects that crawled on their necks, faces and heads. There were clouds of mosquitoes that seemed to hover near their ears creating an insistent drone that made it hard to hear anything else and made the skin on the back of the neck crawl. None of them used insect repellent because the VC could pick up its odor from a long distance. To preserve their concealment, Gerber knew they had to tolerate the mosquitoes and hope the malaria pills worked.

The men let their eyes roam the ground, however, looking for signs of the VC. They watched for movement not caused by the light breeze that did nothing to dry their soaked uniforms or to cool them. And they listened to the night sounds of the jungle, waiting for the misstep that would tell them that the VC were near.

Each of them relaxed as much as possible. Gerber was crouched with one knee on the ground and an elbow resting on the other. It was a position that ensured he wouldn't fall asleep easily. He kept his eyes moving. First he memorized the position of everything that he could see, memorized the shapes of the bushes and the trees and their locations. He checked them frequently, looking for a change that would tell him that the VC had arrived, or that an enemy patrol was passing by or had camped nearby.

It was an hour later that he thought he saw movement among the trees. He watched it carefully, staring off to the side, waiting for it to move again. When it did, he knew the enemy was near. He hoped they would pass him quietly and disappear into the jungle. When the point man of the VC raised a hand and dropped to the ground, Gerber knew that he and his men were in trouble.

15

THE JUNGLE WEST OF
CAMP A-555 NEAR THE
CAMBODIAN BORDER

Keeping his eyes on the VC patrol, Gerber slowly lowered himself to the ground so that he would be harder to spot. He had counted twelve men, each armed with an AK-47. The banana clip, the front sight and bayonet assembly and the pistol grip and short stock gave the weapon a distinct outline.

The VC spread out in a loose ring and collapsed to the ground. None of them moved for ten or fifteen minutes, as if the soldiers were watching the trail behind them, waiting to see if they were being followed. Two then got up and disappeared into the jungle heading south. Another separated from the group, but he didn't seem to have a destination or mission. He strolled casually to where Gerber hid with his face pressed into the dank jungle soil.

The lone VC dropped his trousers and squatted near a small bush. There was a rumbling in his gut and an explosive sound as the odor of rotten eggs drifted toward Gerber. The man seemed to sigh with pleasure but didn't move for several moments. Finally he stripped some of the leaves from the bush, cleaned himself and tossed them away so that they landed next to Gerber's face. Gerber didn't react. His stomach turned over from the pervasive stench, but he didn't move.

The VC finished, stood up and grunted loudly. He bent and jerked his pants up and walked back to his friends, who were now watching him. They were laughing quietly, and there were a few whispered comments.

Gerber waited patiently, the smell from the filthy leaves still hanging near him. With the VC no more than fifteen or twenty yards away from him, he couldn't move. They obviously had not seen him because they had let their discipline lapse.

He had hoped that it was just a short break and that when the two men returned, they would move on. But instead, they seemed to be setting up camp. They dug a small hole, lined it with rocks, then scattered, searching for firewood. A campfire suggested they would remain in place until daylight. Gerber didn't believe they would light the fire at night.

One of the VC came toward Gerber. He stopped and picked up a long crooked stick. He found another larger, shorter one and grabbed it. He stood up, looked at the jungle around him and started to walk directly toward Gerber.

Gerber moved his right hand slowly until he could feel the hilt of his knife. With his thumb he unsnapped the band that held it in place. He kept his hand there and didn't move, didn't breathe. He just waited for the VC to find enough wood and return to his campsite.

But the man kept coming toward him, his arms loaded with wood. He stopped inches from Gerber but didn't look down, his eyes fixed on something else. He began to move again, stepped on Gerber's arm and twisted his ankle. As he stumbled, falling to his knees and dropping the wood, he cried out in pain.

In one fluid motion, Gerber came off the ground with his knife drawn and grabbed the enemy, spinning him. He clamped his hand over the VC's mouth to prevent him from crying out again and drew the blade along the throat from left

to right. There was a splash of blood, a coppery odor, and a
foul stench as the man died. Gerber felt him jerk in a spasm
once, as if trying to kick them both over, and then the man
sagged against him.

Gerber lowered the body to the ground and then crouched
behind it, waiting for the man's yell and ensuing commotion
to draw his friends. For a moment nothing happened. Gerber
reached to his right and touched the stock of his weapon but
didn't pick it up. He didn't want to move any more than he
had to.

There was a whispered call from the VC camp, and then another soldier began to move toward Gerber's position. Behind that man two more appeared. The rest of the enemy were
spread out around the wood-filled hole, watching.

As the VC came nearer, Gerber tensed, prepared to spring
at him. Suddenly a single report erupted in the gloom. The
man's weapon flew upward and outward toward Gerber as he
collapsed to the ground with a grunt of pain and surprise.

At that instant more firing came from behind Gerber, a ripping sound as Fetterman fired, the ruby tracers lashing toward the enemy and the strobelike bursts lighting the ground.
Two of the VC dropped, hit by Fetterman's bullets. Two more
tried to run and were cut down by Krung firing his weapon
single-shot.

Gerber scooped up his weapon and fired rapidly. He hit one
of the fleeing enemy high, either in the shoulder or the back
of the head. The man flipped forward, his feet leaving the
ground. He landed on his face, struggled to sit up and then fell.

Firing broke out to the left. Gerber could see the muzzle-
flashes in the jungle and could hear the bullets snapping overhead. He watched for a moment, aimed his rifle and fired into
the jungle. The return fire, a sustained burst from an AK-47,
forced Gerber down. He pressed his face close to the body of
the man he had knifed. One hand rested in a pool of sticky
blood.

There was a sudden explosion near the point of the enemy firing. Gerber saw a fountain of sparks splash upward as the grenade detonated. There was a shriek of pain, and the firing stopped.

Gerber heard someone crashing through the vegetation. He turned and fired at the sound. Red tracers raked the darkness to his left, but the man kept running.

When the firing died, Gerber moved back to where Fetterman crouched behind a palm log. He leaned close to the master sergeant's ear and whispered, "They know we're here now. At least one of them got away."

"I heard him go," said Fetterman.

"We're going to have to move out. Head closer to Cambodia and then make some good time in the morning."

"I'll get Krung, and we'll take off."

Gerber stared into the darkness where the VC lay. He wanted to check the bodies, see if there was anything on them of intelligence value. He should collect the equipment in order to deny it to the enemy, but he couldn't wait for morning and didn't want to do it in the dark. It was too dangerous, especially with two, maybe three, of the enemy unaccounted for.

Fetterman moved out, heading toward Krung's position. Once the master sergeant had gone a yard, Gerber lost sight of him. He couldn't hear him moving. It was as if Fetterman had vanished in a cloud of smoke. The man was exceptional in the jungle. He could blend into any environment, any terrain, and then spring out before anyone could get near him.

Gerber waited for him to return, watching the VC camp. From somewhere came a quiet moaning sound, as if someone was badly hurt. The moaning rose and fell as the man breathed, sometimes ending with a bubbling cough. But Gerber wasn't going to search for the wounded man. The VC, like their Japanese counterparts in the Second World War, sometimes used the wounded as decoys, getting the Americans to rescue the wounded, or put them out of their misery, and then ambushed them.

Fetterman loomed out of the dark a moment later. He whispered, "Sergeant Krung found the running man and stopped him. Maybe we can hang loose here for a few minutes."

"No, the sound of the firing would alert anyone within a couple of klicks. Besides, two of them left the main body before we had to open fire."

"I find trail near here," Krung said. "We move down it and be far from here."

"No," said Gerber. "Too much of a chance for the VC to set up and wait for us. We can't use any trails for a while, especially after a firefight."

"Then we head off deeper into the jungle," said Fetterman.

"Looks like that is exactly what we do. Krung, you take the point and head due west for a klick. Then stop."

"Sir," said Fetterman. "I probably should hang back a while and see if there is any pursuit. I can catch up later."

"Okay," said Gerber. "Krung, let's go."

Fetterman watched Gerber and Krung disappear into the jungle, moving slowly and quietly to the west. When they were out of sight, Fetterman crawled past the VC camp and found a good hiding place near the base of a large tree. He set his rifle on the ground near it, the operating rod out of the dirt and the barrel slightly elevated. He took his Case fighting knife from the scabbard and settled down to wait.

The moist earth stank with the smell of rotting vegetation. Around him were clouds of mosquitoes that didn't land because his skin was wet with sweat. He could hear some scraping along the branches of the tree just above his head and was sure that it was some kind of snake. He thought he could smell it, too, an odor of ammonia and vinegar. He ignored it because he knew that most snakes would not attack unless cornered. They avoided human beings. The lone exception he knew of was the black mamba, but they lived in Africa, not Southeast Asia.

To the right, hidden by the jungle and the night, was a wounded man. Fetterman could hear his labored breathing. The man seemed to have a sucking chest wound, and the breath rattled in his lungs. It sounded as if the man was quickly drowning in his own blood.

Then he heard the first quiet steps of the returning VC. He knew they would be moving as silently as they could. They would have heard the firefight and would be sneaking back to learn what had happened.

Fetterman shifted slightly. It was an effort to keep his circulation going so that he didn't cramp up at the critical moment. He remained still, glancing right and left, moving only his eyes. He tried not to stare into the jungle.

One of the men came forward slowly, his weapon held in both hands, the bayonet extended. He moved from the cover of a bush to the side of a tree. He passed Fetterman, the hole where the firewood had been dumped and then moved deeper into the jungle.

The second man appeared then. He came forward in a slight crouch. He kept away from the trees where Fetterman hid, looked at the fire pit and then stumbled over a body. He said nothing, put out a hand to break his fall and made almost no noise.

At that instant Fetterman sprang from his hiding place with a catlike motion, clapped a hand over the VC's nose and mouth and drove the blade of his knife up through the man's kidney and into his left lung. Fetterman felt the man's blood spill, covering his hand.

He pulled the enemy backward and slashed the knife across his throat, severing the larynx from the trachea and cutting both carotid arteries. The hot blood spurted weakly, soaking the front of Fetterman's uniform. Quietly he laid the body on the ground, pulled the AK from the slack fingers and set it on the jungle floor out of the VC's reach.

Suddenly the first man appeared almost beside Fetterman but apparently didn't see him. Fetterman stood and turned, driving in his knife to the hilt just above the enemy's web belt, ripping upward until he hit the breastbone. A stench from the VC's bowels rose from the wound to assault Fetterman's nostrils.

The man had tried to jump back at the first hint of pain, but Fetterman held him. The VC dropped his rifle and reached around, feeling his guts spilling from the gaping hole in his stomach. He started to scream, a high-pitched whine that Fetterman ended by slashing the throat. The man fell to the jungle floor and drummed a sandaled foot on the soft ground as he died.

Fetterman quickly moved away from the dead man. He wiped the blade of his knife on his sleeve. He slipped it into the scabbard and then picked up his rifle. As he crossed the ambush site, he wished there was something he could do about the weapons. There were ten or twelve AKs lying in the dirt that could be of use to the VC if they found them soon enough.

He grinned to himself, and moved back to the ambush. He found one of the AKs, depressed the lever at the back of the bolt and lifted off the guard on the top of the weapon. He took the bolt out, released a couple of pins and had the trigger housing in his hand. With an underhand throw he scattered the parts and dropped the AK to the ground. During the next ten minutes he located several other of the weapons and took the bolts, putting them into his pack before tossing the other pieces around. Now even if the VC found the weapons, they would have to be repaired, and if the VC didn't find them for a day or two, most of the weapons should have a terminal case of rust, he thought.

With that finished he headed off to the west to find Krung and Captain Gerber. It didn't take him long to catch up to them.

AT DAWN THEY WERE at the edge of the jungle, looking at a wide expanse of open fields and rice paddies that swept from them into Cambodia. It was broken by a sliver of jungle that dipped into it about half a klick away. To the north was a solid expanse of jungle. A klick to the south was a clump of palm trees that shaded a farmer's hootch. Smoke rose from it, but they could see no one moving near it. Beyond that was swamp. Overhead a jet streaked high, just a flash of silver in the bright blue cloudless sky.

Gerber sat with his back to a tree, eating peaches from an OD C-ration can. Fetterman and Krung were watching for the enemy while Gerber relaxed. In ten minutes he would change places with Krung so that the Tai striker could eat his cold breakfast. Later it would be Fetterman's turn.

When he finished, Gerber buried the can in a shallow hole, threw in the remains of the bread and jelly he hadn't finished, then drank from his canteen. This time he didn't finish the water right away. He would wait until they prepared to move.

Before Gerber could get up, Fetterman was near him. "We've got more company."

"Now what?"

"I think we've got a party of VC spotted about half a klick from here. They're flirting with the edge of the jungle off to the north, so I can't be sure."

"They're not Cavanaugh's men, are they?"

"No, sir, I don't think so. I'm not sure who they are. They could be a bunch of farmers trying to get an early start, although I think that a couple of them are carrying weapons."

"You know," Gerber said, "I can't recall when we've found more people running around this AO. Everyone and his brother."

"Yes, sir."

Gerber got up. "Why don't you show me these guys."

Fetterman led him to the edge of the jungle, but the line of people had disappeared, having diverted into the trees. Krung pointed to the last place he had seen them and told them that the men had turned to the north.

"Then I guess we go to plan two," Gerber announced.

"Which is?"

"Krung, take a break. We'll keep watch," said Gerber.

As Krung eased away from the edge of the jungle, Gerber noticed another group of men who seemed to be following the line of march of the first bunch. Gerber used the scope on his rifle to study them. They wore a mixed bag of uniforms and clothes—some black pajamas, some fatigues, but almost every one of them wore one of the American boonie hats.

Fetterman used his binoculars. He crawled closer to Gerber. "That second group could be Sean's men. I think I recognize one or two of them."

"Christ, Tony, you don't think we've lucked into something, do you?"

"I can't see Sean," said Fetterman. "Wait a minute. Wait a fucking minute. There he is."

"Where?" said Gerber. He flipped the safety off his weapon.

"At the end of the column. There's a big mahogany tree sticking up there. See it?"

"Got it."

"Cavanaugh just passed it."

"Yeah. Got him." Gerber crouched behind a log, using it as a support for his rifle.

"I make the range just over six hundred meters, Captain."

Gerber hit the magazine release. He dropped it to the ground and dug out the one that had eight rounds in it, the special rounds that Fetterman and Tyme had loaded. He jammed the magazine home and worked the bolt, ejecting the round that was already chambered.

"Not much wind, Captain. Light breeze blowing from left to right."

Gerber put the cross hairs on Cavanaugh's chest. He could see the sergeant's face, almost see the color of his eyes. There were sweat stains on his fatigues, and Gerber had the impression that Cavanaugh could use a shave. And the impression that Cavanaugh was very young. That was the thing that stuck in his mind. Cavanaugh was young, not yet twenty years old.

All that through a telescopic sight? Gerber knew that he was letting his mind run loose. There was no way he could get an impression of Cavanaugh's youth through the scope. No way he could tell that the sergeant needed a shave. Gerber's mind was filling in the details.

Cavanaugh disappeared for a moment, stepping behind a tree. He reappeared, and Gerber moved the cross hairs so that he would lead Sean by several feet, gauging the speed of the group's march. He let out his breath, took another, exhaled and began to squeeze the trigger.

The burst of AK fire slammed into the log just as Gerber pulled the trigger. He jerked the trigger, throwing the round off. He had no idea where it went.

Fetterman spun and shot into the sound. He saw a single VC jump to the left, rolling behind a tree. Fetterman slipped to his right, trying to flank the enemy.

There was a single shot from the right, near the location where Krung had been eating. Krung appeared then, holding up the AK-47.

"Captain?" said Fetterman.

"Looks like we've walked into something. Krung, any indication of others out there?"

Before Krung could answer, shooting broke out around them. Bullets clipped the leaves of the trees, showering them. Several rounds slammed into a nearby tree, stripping the bark from it. More shooting came from the right, as if the enemy was moving toward them in a semicircular formation designed to box them in. Gerber couldn't flee across the paddy fields now behind them. It was too open.

Gerber caught a flash and sighted through the scope. He could see the enemy soldier so clearly that it looked as if the man was no more than four or five feet away. He could see the scar on the chin, the light mustache and the thin eyebrows. The man wore a pith helmet pushed back on his head so that Gerber could make out the jet-black hair.

He set the cross hairs on the center of the man's chest and pulled the trigger. A hole appeared in the man's chest and the dust flew from his shirt. He even had time to see the surprised expression on the man's face as he dropped his rifle and lifted his hands. Blood spurted, the stream nearly three feet long as the VC turned and fell.

To the right, Gerber could see part of a VC's head as the man peeked around a tree, firing his weapon without aiming it. He was spraying bullets in Fetterman's direction. Gerber put the cross hairs on the man's eye, a brown bloodshot eye, and pulled the trigger. The side of the enemy's face disintegrated in a spray of blood and bone. He didn't seem to react. He just dropped from sight.

"Captain," Fetterman yelled. "Coming up from behind us."

Gerber turned and saw two dozen of the enemy, dressed in black pajamas, web gear and sandals. Gerber opened fire on them, shooting as quickly as he could pull the trigger. He ran out of ammo, quickly dropped the magazine and slammed a spare one home. He put the cross hairs on a man, fired and saw the VC go down in a loose-jointed fashion.

Fetterman was firing on full automatic. He dropped three of the VC. Two of them tumbled forward into a dry paddy and didn't move. The other fell back, disappearing behind a dike.

Fetterman aimed at another man, picked him off easily and fired at a fifth.

To the left, Krung was busy shooting at the shadows. Men would appear, squeeze off a couple of rounds and then dive for cover. A Chicom grenade bounced off the tree next to him. Krung dived for cover as it detonated, the shrapnel burying itself in the trees around them. Krung looked up in time to see two men rushing him. The Tai striker dropped them both with a short burst. One of them fell nearly at his feet, tried to get up and then Krung put a round into his face.

Gerber heard noise to his right. He turned from the rice paddies and saw a man running through the jungle. He snapped a shot at him, missed and tried again. The second round buried itself in the trunk of a tree. Gerber waited, saw the man again and fired. The round again slammed into a tree near the man's head.

"Damn!" Gerber swore. He caught a flash out of the corner of his eye and saw another enemy. Before he could fire, the man opened up, his round smashing into the log near Gerber. Gerber rolled right, fired and rolled again. He heard the man fall into the jungle.

Fetterman reloaded his weapon. Most of the VCs in front of him had taken cover behind the rice paddies. He raked the top of one, the bullets kicking the dirt high in dark brown geysers. There was a shout, and two men leaped up to throw grenades. Fetterman's burst caught one in the stomach as his arm snapped forward. The VC lost the grip on his weapon, tossing it four or five feet in front of him. He disappeared in a cloud of dust and shrapnel thrown up in the explosion.

The other man threw his grenade as hard as he could before he dropped behind the safety of his dike. The grenade hit the ground in front of Fetterman and bounced once toward him. Fetterman fielded it in his bare hand like a third baseman picking up a slow roller. He threw it back and dropped to the jungle floor. As soon as he heard the explosion, he was up again, firing at the enemy as they exposed themselves.

At that moment the area around them seemed to erupt. There was shooting from AKs and at least one RPD. The bullets formed an almost impenetrable wall of lead that stripped leaves from trees, chopped the tops off small trees, toppling them, and shredded the bark from the palms and teaks.

Gerber rolled next to his log. He felt the impact of bullets slamming into it. He listened to the whine and buzz of the slugs as they ricocheted off rocks on the jungle floor. There was a shout from the jungle and an answer from the rice paddies. A bugle call ripped through the noise, a wailing note that built in volume like the siren of a police car. A whistle sounded but was quickly overpowered by the voices of the enemy. They were screaming and yelling at one another as they suddenly left the protection of the jungle trees or the rice paddy dikes, rushing toward the three men.

Gerber looked up and saw four men coming at him. He jerked his rifle around and fired from the hip. One man spun, the round slamming into his shoulder. The head of a second disappeared in an explosion of crimson as the body kept coming at him. The third man was almost on him as Gerber rolled right, braced his back against the log and got to his knees. He fired, but the bullet seemed to have no effect on the enemy soldier.

The man tried to stick his bayonet into Gerber's chest. Gerber parried the blade with his rifle, shoving it to the side. He swung the butt of the rifle around, smashing the man's face. He came back around, the barrel of his rifle pointed at the last VC. The man tried to slam his rifle butt into Gerber's face. Gerber blocked it with his own weapon, shattering the scope. Gerber hit him with the barrel, and as the man fell, Gerber put three rounds into him, the blood splashing over him, staining his uniform.

Gerber spun, saw two men in the rice paddy and fired once. The bolt of his weapon locked back, and Gerber snatched at the ammo pouch on his pistol belt. He let the empty magazine fall from his weapon, slapped the new one home and released the bolt as the two men leaped the last dike before they got to the trees. Gerber fired rapidly, and both men died, blood blossoming on their chests.

The firing around them seemed to peak in a roar that blended the individual weapons into a single continuous explosion. Gerber felt something tug at his shoulder and spin him. He fell forward and threw out his hands to break his fall. He thought he'd been hit but didn't feel any pain. There was no sudden warm wetness and no flare of white-hot pain. He picked up his weapon and opened fire again, ignoring the dull ache.

But the VC were retreating. A couple of them were running to the rear, toward a narrow strip of jungle on the other side of the paddies, north of the swamps. One of them took a round in the back. He dived forward, his arms outstretched, belly flopping into the dirt of a dry paddy. His friend glanced at him but kept running. He tossed his AK away and then unbuckled his web gear, shrugging it from his shoulders without breaking stride.

There was covering fire from one of the RPDs. A grenade exploded in the center of a paddy near them, the cloud of red dust obscuring the retreating men but too far away to injure them. The shooting tapered rapidly until it was only sporadic firing.

Then from the north came the sounds of a sustained battle. It sounded as if the men with Cavanaugh had either caught the VC moving there or had stumbled over them, starting the firefight.

Fetterman moved closer to Gerber. "Captain? You okay?"

Gerber rubbed his shoulder and then glanced down. The bullet had hit him high on the scabbard, which was taped to his web gear. It had shattered the tip of the knife, ricocheted off without penetrating the scabbard or the thick material of the harness.

His shoulder was sore, and he was certain it would be badly bruised, but that was better than having a bullet hole in it. He grinned at Fetterman. "I'm fine," he reassured the master sergeant.

Krung backed up toward them, his rifle pointing at the jungle. He kept his eyes moving, watching the trees, waiting for the VC to come at them again.

"Captain, we've got to get out of here," urged Fetterman. "This isn't the best position in the world."

"And we're going to run out of ammo," added Gerber. He looked at the men lying on the jungle floor close to them. They carried AKs and had extra ammo with them. Gerber and his men could always use that.

"We could try to work our way toward Cavanaugh's men," Fetterman suggested. "Join up with them."

"And then what?" asked Gerber. "Just shoot Cavanaugh once the VC have been eliminated."

"No, sir," Fetterman answered. "But we'd better do something fast, or we're not going to survive until lunch."

16

THE JUNGLE WEST OF
CAMP A-555

Before Gerber could respond, firing broke out again all around them. Fetterman leaped to the left, rolling for cover near a palm tree. He opened up as the VC swarmed from the jungle across the rice paddies, screaming and shooting. Green tracers, burning dimly in the bright morning sunshine, flashed into the jungle or bounced off the ground, arcing skyward.

Gerber dived for the protection of his log, laid the barrel of his M-14 on it and began shooting rapidly. The smashed scope was useless, so Gerber aimed by looking along the barrel. He saw two men go down, but there were so many of them now. Not just VC in black pajamas, but NVA wearing full uniforms of deep green and khaki pith helmets. The men were running across the open ground, leaping the rice paddy dikes as if they were hurdles in a race.

From the apex of the sliver of jungle, due west of Gerber's position, an NVA machine gun opened fire, raking the jungle around them with 7.62 mm rounds.

And from behind them came another shout, orders in high-pitched Vietnamese as the firing there began again. Gerber heard the flatter reports of Krung's weapon as he tried to stop the enemy from overrunning them.

At that moment Gerber knew it was all over. There were too many of the enemy coming too fast, and even if all three of them had machine guns, they wouldn't be able to stop the Vietcong and the NVA. There was no time to call for artillery or air support because the enemy was too close. If the attack slowed or there was a momentary retreat, he might be able to shout for help. Now all he could do was fight. Gerber tossed his empty M-14 to the side and grabbed one of the AKs near him. He flipped the selector to full auto and pulled the trigger. He emptied the weapon and scrambled over to the body to find more ammunition.

Suddenly another machine gun joined the firing, but this one seemed to be raking the onrushing enemy. A dozen of them fell in a hail of bullets. The others turned, firing at the five men who were attacking them. One held an M-60 at his hip, a belt of ammo across his shoulder, and was running at them, firing short bursts. As he got closer to them, the enemy began returning fire, the bullets kicking up the dirt all around him. He dived for cover in the corner of a rice paddy and started shooting again.

The enemy seemed to forget about Gerber and his tiny party. They turned their assault, attacking the machine gun and the men who supported it, but the machine gunner kept up a steady fire until the bolt of his weapon locked back as the belt broke.

FROM FAR TO THE RIGHT came a single burst of AK fire. Sean Cavanaugh reacted to it by diving for cover among the trees. At that moment the VC patrol that he had been shadowing with nearly three dozen of his men scattered in the trees. The two forces, separated by a hundred meters or more, jockeyed for position, moving toward one another, until Cavanaugh saw one of the black-clad enemy hunched over, an SKS clutched in his hands, running along a narrow jungle trail. Cavanaugh aimed and squeezed off a round. The man took the slug in the chest, staggered two steps and fell among some small bushes.

Firing broke out all around him. The strikers formed a skirmish line and waited for the VC to rush them. They poured rifle and machine-gun fire into the jungle and punctuated it with M-79 rounds.

Cavanaugh worked his way forward, crawling along the moist ground. He could hear the enemy rounds passing over his head. There was an acrid stink of gunpowder hanging in the air around him. He kept his elbows and knees moving until he was at the edge of the trail, but he could see nothing of the enemy. Their return fire had tapered to an occasional shot or short burst from an AK. They were trying to break contact.

Then to his left he heard more shooting. Machine guns and AKs against M-14s. He pulled back until he was behind his skirmish line and then got to his feet, running to the edge of the jungle. He saw more of the VC and the NVA running across the open ground, firing into the jungle south of him. Some of them fell, hit by the fire pouring from the jungle. The enemy didn't hesitate, but kept the pressure on the unidentified men in the jungle. From a sliver of jungle that stuck out into the rice paddy, an RPD opened up.

The attack seemed to falter as the men trapped among the trees took a heavy toll of the attackers. Cavanaugh watched them fall, tumbling into the dry paddies. He looked at his strikers and changed the skirmish line so that it was covering his back.

The enemy started another surging charge across the rice paddies. Cavanaugh grabbed the handle on the top of the M-60, draped a belt of ammo over his shoulder and shouted, ''Let's go.''

He ran from the trees, sprinting across the dry paddies, heading toward the flank of the NVA. He fired a short burst that took them by surprise. Several of them fell as the bullets slammed into them. A squad seemed to peel from the attackers, changing direction, firing at Cavanaugh's small force.

Cavanaugh leaped into the corner of a rice paddy, sliding to the ground. He pushed the barrel of his weapon over the top, aimed and began a hammering fire that tore holes in the NVA line. The RPD that had been shooting into the trees suddenly raked the ground near Cavanaugh, trying to force him to take cover, but Cavanaugh ignored the bullets kicking up the dirt around him. He let the four strikers with him turn their weapons on the enemy machine gun. One of them was lobbing M-79 grenades at the RPD, but the rounds were falling short.

The belt of ammo feeding the M-60 broke as the links separated. Cavanaugh flipped up the top, jammed the rounds back in and worked the bolt, but the weapon failed to fire. He cocked it again and again and pulled the trigger. It fired three rounds, then jammed, and Cavanaugh worked to clear it as the VC and NVA got closer to him.

The strikers fired into the onrushing mass, knocking some of them down, but the enemy kept coming, shooting from the hip. The whole force changed the point of their attack, forgetting about the men hidden in the jungle. Cavanaugh got the M-60 working again, but the enemy was too close.

The sergeant leaped to meet the onslaught. He grabbed the barrel of the weapon, burning his hands as he swung it like a baseball bat. He felt the solid impact as the receiver group crushed the head of an enemy soldier. He swung it back and forth in a widening arc as the VC danced in and out, trying to use their bayonets and knives.

Around him the strikers were in a death struggle. They used their weapons as clubs, hammering at the VC and the NVA, using the tricks that Cavanaugh had taught them. They screamed at the enemy, trying to force them from their tiny perimeter. One by one they died, a bullet in the head, a bayonet through the neck, or the chest, or the stomach. A dozen wounds that proved fatal and caused their blood to stain the dry ground around them. All went down within a few minutes of one another until only Cavanaugh was left alive.

He threw the machine gun at one of the VC, knocking the man to the ground. He jumped back and grabbed at a handle in the pack belonging to one of the dead strikers, ripping the entrenching tool free. He swung it with all his might. He hit a man in the shoulder and heard the bones break.

He swung again, catching an NVA soldier in the side of the head. The pith helmet flew off as the E-tool opened a gash that exposed the man's brain. The enemy fell, both hands on his head, screaming as his feet kicked spasmodically.

There was a sharp blow to the E-tool, a bullet bouncing off it. In that moment Cavanaugh felt he was invincible. He couldn't be killed because he led a charmed life. He could stand in the middle of a firefight and the bullets would pass him harmlessly. He was a super soldier who would inflict such losses on the enemy that they would quit the war.

He leaped to the top of the dike, challenging the VC. He swung the E-tool downward and clubbed one of the NVA. Blood splattered as the man's head caved in. Cavanaugh laughed as he swung again, missed a man who ducked, leaning toward him. Cavanaugh snapped a foot out and caught the man in the chin, breaking it as the teeth shattered.

Cavanaugh laughed again as the VC and the NVA backed up, almost as if they were in awe of him. As if they couldn't believe the man they were facing, the bodies of their dead ringing him.

Cavanaugh feinted to the left and then came right, the edge of the tool slicing into the belly of a man, spilling his guts. Cavanaugh swung upward so that the blade hit the man under the chin, dropping him on his back.

"I'm invincible!" he shouted. He stared at the men around him, his eyes blazing with a strange light. "Come on! You can't kill me!"

For a moment he was lost in the half light that had surrounded the listening post. He saw the bodies of Sergeant Luong and Corporal Lim, the remains of the field phone and the PRC-10 that had been riddled by enemy fire. He heard the pop of the mortars as they threw illumination rounds into the sky over the listening post and wondered why the battle went on forever. A battle that he won time and time again but one that he had to fight time and time again.

He grunted with the effort of swinging the E-tool, snapping his wrists as it connected with a man's body. He heard the man groan under the impact.

As Cavanaugh spun, he felt something strike his side. He heard the wet smack as the bullet punched through him and felt a white-hot flare of pain. It didn't bother him because he knew that it was only a momentary annoyance, and then it would be healed. He would continue to crush the enemy until they were all dead, lying in heaps around him, or until they fled the field.

There was a second pain, high on his shoulder, and the bright sunlight began to dim, as if clouds had suddenly obscured it. Cavanaugh didn't realize that he had dropped the E-tool. He thought that he still stood on the rice paddy dike, the makeshift weapon in his hand. He thought that he was still killing the enemy.

Around him he heard shooting and was relieved because it meant that this time the strikers were the ones who had come back to life, the dead soldiers who had been animated by some unseen and unknown force. This time Cavanaugh wouldn't be left alone on the field of the dead. He would have company.

A third bullet hit him in the stomach, and he fell to his knees. He turned slightly to the left and toppled off the dike, landing on his back in the paddy. He was staring up at the sun. It seemed to be no brighter than the evening star. He wondered what had happened to it and what was happening around him. He could hear random firing and shouting in Vietnamese. He felt a tug at his pistol belt and thought that he raised a hand to slap at the man who touched him.

As the blackness closed in around him, he knew that he was the ultimate soldier. He had been born with the world, had fought in all its campaigns and would not die until the last shot in the last war was fired. Then he would grow old rapidly and fade from the landscape.

GERBER CONTINUED to pour fire from his AK into the rice paddies, shooting the VC and the NVA quickly. The bodies began to pile in heaps near the man who, miraculously, hadn't gone down. Cavanaugh had tossed away the machine gun, which had been broken and bent, and was using an entrenching tool to defend himself.

Gerber lost sight of him as a crowd of NVA swarmed over the paddy dike. He saw more of them fall and then heard shouting to the north.

Twenty men rushed from the tree line, racing over the open ground, screaming and shooting until they were mixed with the enemy. Some of them fell as the VC began to return fire, and then the shooting tapered to an occasional shot in the hand-to-hand fighting.

Gerber turned his attention to the VC in the jungle with him. He saw two of them and fired, the rounds slamming into a tree near them. Fetterman did the same, helping Krung drive the VC from them. The sudden increase in shooting pushed the Vietcong back.

As the VC among the trees retreated, Gerber turned his attention to the battle in the rice paddies. The NVA and the VC there were fleeing, too, forced back by the attacking strikers. The strikers swarmed over the rice paddy where Cavanaugh lay, took firing positions and raked the enemy with a devastating fusillade.

The VC and the NVA raced for safety. Once the men gained the trees, the machine gun fell silent. There was some random sniping that quickly died down. It was as if the enemy was fighting a rear guard action, and once the majority of the soldiers escaped into Cambodia, the rear guard faded from sight.

Gerber spent an hour watching the jungle, the rice paddies, and the men who were crouched among the dikes in front of him. He had contacted his base with the order to have an artillery barrage ready in case the enemy reappeared. They had fired a couple of marking rounds from Fire Support Base Custer and then said they would stand by, but the enemy didn't reappear. Fetterman circulated through the jungle around them, checking the bodies of the dead VC, stripping them of their weapons and ammo and searching for insignia, documents and anything else that would be of value to Intelligence.

It was clear that the VC and the NVA had left the field. They had tried for a quick victory, and when that failed, they had withdrawn, fearing that the Americans and the South Vietnamese would use the daylight hours to mount a large-scale assault.

Gerber picked up the broken XM-21. He jerked the sniperscope from the top and dropped it to the jungle floor. He worked the bolt, made sure that a round was chambered and then moved to the edge of the jungle. When he was joined by Fetterman and Krung, he stepped out into the open and walked slowly toward the rice paddy where the strikers waited.

As he neared them, he recognized some of them. They stood waiting for him, their eyes on the ground. He could see that they had gathered the bodies of their dead and covered them with poncho liners. He stopped at the dike and studied the ground around him, staring at the dead men scattered there.

Without a word to the strikers, Gerber moved to the body that had to be an American. He pulled the cover away and stared at the peaceful look on Cavanaugh's face. It was a look of contentment that suggested he knew exactly what he had been doing and didn't care that it would kill him. It was what he had wanted. He had come a long way to find it.

Thoughts swirled in Gerber's mind. Thoughts about Cavanaugh and what he had done. Taking the war to the enemy and fighting them as a guerrilla force made more sense than establishing a line of forts to watch the frontier. That hadn't worked during the Indian Wars, and it wouldn't work now. The hostiles hadn't been subdued until the Army left the relative comfort of its warm forts and chased the Indians across the plains, using the tactics that the Indians themselves used. Maybe Cavanaugh understood on some unconscious level that the VC and the NVA would never be defeated by an Army that built large base camps, then found excuses to stay behind the wire.

Or maybe Cavanaugh's mind had snapped. He hadn't been able to take all the killing, hadn't been able to take all the death that seemed to serve no useful purpose because the accomplishment of yesterday was wiped out by the decisions made tomorrow. No progress was made toward ending the war, but the men still died.

There had been no real reason for Cavanaugh to attack the enemy across the open ground. He could have stayed among the trees and fired on them. The range was long, but it wouldn't have made that much of a difference. His reckless assault had saved the lives of Gerber, Fetterman and Krung. There was no question of that.

Fetterman, who was standing next to Gerber, asked, "Now what?"

"We collect the bodies and move them to a more defensible position."

"What about the strikers here?" asked Fetterman.

"I would think that's Minh's problem. They're his men. If he wants to count them AWOL, then that's his privilege. If he wants to punish them for their part in all this, it's up to him."

"And Sean?" asked Fetterman quietly.

"Sean was involved in two earlier actions that rated the Medal of Honor. There were no witnesses to either of those. I think this one rates it, too, and we both witnessed it. He sacrificed himself to save us."

"Captain," said Fetterman, "I don't think he knew we were here. He only saw the enemy and rushed in to kill them."

"Cavanaugh realized that we were about to be overrun and exposed himself to enemy gunners in an attempt to draw their attention away from us. His heroic act is the sole reason that we survived after being caught in an enemy ambush."

"Yes, sir," Fetterman agreed. "If he hadn't charged from the trees and almost single-handedly turned back a large-scale combined VC and NVA assault, we would have died. Even after being severely wounded himself, he continued the attack. It was a most impressive feat of arms."

Gerber pointed at the bodies, counting rapidly, and then doubled the figure. "When we finally reached his position, there were thirty-two enemy soldiers lying dead around him. In the end Cavanaugh had used his entrenching tool to fight them off."

"Yes, sir," said Fetterman. "An impressive piece of fighting. You think we'll have any trouble getting this one through?"

"I doubt it. And you and I have been around long enough to know *how* to write up the citation. The act becomes secondary to that. It is how it is presented that counts."

Fetterman turned and stared at the captain. "You think this is the right thing to do? Trying to get him the Medal of Honor like this? Won't it cheapen the award?"

"Tony, did Sean deserve it for the defense of the listening post?"

"Yes, sir. He certainly did."

"Then all we're doing is ensuring that he gets it. Maybe he doesn't deserve it for this action, but he does for defending his listening post. Not to mention that patrol that was wiped out."

"Yes, sir."

"Now let's get things organized and get the fuck out of here."

17

THE TEAM HOUSE,
CAMP A-555

Gerber sat in the team house, his feet propped on one of the tables, his ankles crossed. He held a can of warm beer in one hand and the *Stars and Stripes* in the other. He had read on the front page that there had been demonstrations in Da Nang, that McNamara had announced the new troop ceiling at nearly a quarter of a million men and that B-52s were being employed in the bombing of the North.

Flipping the paper over to the back page, he found a small story that acknowledged the completion of Operation Blue Star, a body recovery detail that had returned to Camp A-102 about two weeks after the battle there. The North Vietnamese had deserted the camp, leaving two hundred unburied dead scattered across the battlefield. The locals had stayed away, fearing ghosts, and the graves registration party had found that the bodies were reduced to skeletons. They had found watches, still running, attached to the wristbones of the dead Americans. And they had learned that someone, a brave someone, had gotten into the arms room and destroyed all the classified documents before the North Vietnamese could get them.

Gerber stared at the story for a long time. He wasn't sure what it was about it that bothered him. Maybe it was the description of the bodies reduced to skeletons wearing watches that continued to run. Maybe it was the mention of a skeletal hand clutching a .45, grass growing between the bones of the wrist and hand. He didn't know.

He dropped his feet to the floor and drained his beer. He tossed the can at the bin next to the refrigerator that held the empties and opened the paper.

As he looked into the center of the newspaper, he felt his stomach turn over. There was a picture of Sean Cavanaugh, looking as if he had just escaped from high school, smiling out at him. Gerber stared at the young face, short hair and the white shirt and dark tie of a young man who had graduated from high school, evaded the draft by volunteering for active duty in the Army and found himself in Vietnam almost before anyone in the World knew where in the hell it was.

Below the picture of Cavanaugh was another of two people. Gerber had thought of Cavanaugh's parents as elderly, but these people didn't look old. They looked miserable. The woman, who had long, light-colored hair, held a handkerchief to her face as the man, his mouth turned down, the tears obvious on his face even in the black-and-white photo, accepted the Congressional Medal of Honor from the President. The medal, a scrap of powder blue cloth sprinkled with white stars, and a chunk of iron formed into a wreath with a star in the center and the word Valor engraved on it, was certainly not worth a son.

Gerber didn't need to read the story because he knew what it would say. Knew all too well because he had read a dozen, a hundred others. It would mention that the parents of Sean Cavanaugh were presented the medal in a small ceremony at the White House. "Sergeant Cavanaugh, on or about 2 April 1966, did distinguish himself . . ."

Gerber folded the paper and set it on the table so that he could stare at the photos. Although it was hot outside and the ceiling fan spinning over his head did nothing to alleviate the heat, Gerber was suddenly cold. A clammy sweat dripped down his sides.

Another strange contrast. The death of a Special Forces camp in the A Shau Valley and the death of a Special Forces sergeant near Cambodia. One buried on the back page of the *Stars and Stripes* so that the men who needed the information would have it, and the other featured prominently so that the men who needed the encouragement would have it.

He got up and walked to the refrigerator. He opened it, removed a cool beer and used the church key that was kept on top of the refrigerator to open the beverage. He took a deep swallow and remembered. He glanced over at the open newspaper and remembered.

Remembered Bates telling him, "I don't care what he did out there. He was a deserter, and I don't think he rates the Medal of Honor."

Gerber had listened to Bates explain, at great length, what the medal stood for. Explain that the men who earned it had done extraordinary things that defied the imagination. Men who had risked their lives, who had lost their lives, rescuing their friends, turning back enemy assaults with staggering losses, who had been wounded, two three, five times and still directed the battle or carried friends to safety. Men who defied the odds.

All through Bates's explanation Gerber had listened and then said quietly, "You mean like defending a listening post when all your friends are dead and there is no ammo. Defending it with the butt of a broken carbine and a bloody entrenching tool. Leaving nearly seventy dead VC around it."

Bates had rocked back in his chair, stared at his desktop for a long time and then said, "Yeah. Exactly like that."

"We didn't do right by Cavanaugh," Gerber said. "We should have pushed for his medal then. We should have visited him in the hospital. The list of what we should have done is so long that it reaches from here to Cambodia. We all stepped on our dicks on this one, and getting him the Medal of Honor now won't make up for it, but it'll make his parents feel a little better. He deserves it."

"All right, Mack, put in the papers. Get the citations written up and signed and notarized, and I'll take them to General Hull. He knows what's going on. He's been around long enough to understand. I'm sure he'll forward it with a recommendation for approval."

And now Gerber was reading that the President had given the medal to Cavanaugh's parents. Held the ceremony in the Rose Garden on a sunny afternoon with a lot of brass from the Pentagon standing around listening and saluting. Gerber looked at the table, at the photos that were blurry now, and took a deep drink of his beer.

"Yeah!" he said. "You deserved it."

GLOSSARY

AC—Aircraft Commander. Pilot in charge of an aircraft.

AFVN—Armed Forces radio and television network in Vietnam. Army PFC Pat Sajak was probably the most memorable of AFVN's DJs with his loud and long "Goooooooooooood Morning, Vietnam!" The Spinning Wheel of Fortune gives no clues about his whereabouts today.

AK-47—Selective fire assault rifle used by the NVA and the VC. It fired the same ammunition as the SKS carbine, which was used early in the war. The AK-47 replaced it.

AN/PRC-10—Portable radio. Also called Prick-10.

AN/PRC-25—Became the standard infantry radio used in Vietnam. Sometimes called Prick-25.

AO—Area of Operation.

AP ROUNDS—Armor-piercing ammunition.

ARVN—Army of the Republic of Vietnam. South Vietnamese soldier. Also known as Marvin Arvin.

ASH AND TRASH—Single ship flights by helicopters taking care of a variety of missions, such as flying cargo, supplies, mail and people among the various small camps in Vietnam, for anyone who needed aviation support.

BAR—.30-caliber Browning Automatic Rifle.

BEAUCOUP—Many.

BISCUIT—C-rations. Combat rations.

BLOWER—See *Horn*.

BODY COUNT—Number of enemy killed, wounded or captured during an operation. Used by Saigon and Washington as a means of measuring the progress of the war.

BOOM-BOOM—Term used by Vietnamese prostitutes to sell their product.

BOONDOGGLE—Any military operation that hasn't been completely thought out. An operation that is ridiculous.

BOONIE HATS—Soft cap worn by the grunts in the field when not wearing a steel pot.

BUSHMASTER—Jungle warfare expert or soldier highly skilled in jungle navigation and combat. Also a large deadly snake not common to Vietnam but mighty tasty.

C AND C—Command and Control aircraft that circled overhead to direct the combined air and ground operations.

CARIBOU—Twin-engine cargo transport plane; C-123.

CHINOOK—Army Aviation twin-engine helicopter. CH-47. Shit hook.

CHURCH KEY—Beer can opener used in the days before pop tops.

CLAYMORE—Antipersonnel mine that fires 750 steel balls with a lethal range of 50 meters.

CLOSE AIR SUPPORT—Use of airplanes and helicopters to fire on enemy units near friendly troops.

CMH—Congressional Medal of Honor.

CO CONG—Female Vietcong soldier.

DAI UY—Vietnamese Army rank equivalent to U.S. Army Captain.

DCI—Director, Central Intelligence. Director of the CIA.

DEROS—Date of Estimated Return From Overseas Service.

DONG—Unit of North Vietnamese money about equal to an American penny.

FIIGMO—Fuck It, I've Got My Orders.

FIVE—Radio call sign for the Executive Officer of a unit.

FNG—Fucking New Guy.

FRENCH FORT—Distinctive, triangular structure built by the hundreds throughout Vietnam by the French.

FUBAR—Fucked Up Beyond All Recognition.

GARAND—M-1 rifle, which was replaced by the M-14. Issued to the Vietnamese early in the war.

GO-TO-HELL RAG—Towel or any large cloth worn around the neck by grunts to absorb perspiration, clean their weapons and dry their hands.

GRUNT—Infantryman.

GUARD THE RADIO—To stand by in the communications bunker and listen for incoming messages.

GUNSHIP—Armed helicopter or cargo plane that carries weapons instead of cargo.

HE—High-explosive ammunition.

HOOTCH—Almost any shelter, from temporary to long-term.

HORN—Specific radio communications network in Vietnam that used satellites to rebroadcast messages.

HORSE—See *Biscuit*.

HOTEL THREE—Helicopter landing area at Saigon's Tan Son Nhut Air Force Base.

HUEY—Bell helicopter. Slick. Called a Huey because its original designation was HU, but it was later changed to UH.

IN-COUNTRY—American troops operating in South Vietnam were all in-country.

INTELLIGENCE—Any information about enemy operations, including troop movements, weapons capabilities, biographies of enemy commanders and general information about terrain features. It is any information that could be useful in planning a mission. Also refers to the branch of the military that specifically deals with the gathering of such information.

KABAR—Military combat knife.

KIA—Killed In Action. Since the U.S. was not engaged in a declared war, the use of KIA was not authorized. KIA came to mean enemy dead. Americans were KHA or Killed In Hostile Action.

KLICK—One thousand meters. Kilometer.

LEGS—Derogatory term for regular infantry used by airborne qualified troops.

LIMA LIMA—Land line. Telephone communications between two points on the ground.

LLDB—Luc Luong Dac Biet. South Vietnamese Special Forces. Sometimes referred to as the Look Long, Duck Back.

LP—Listening Post. Position outside the perimeter manned by a couple of soldiers to warn of enemy activity.

LZ—Landing Zone.

M-14—Standard rifle of the U.S. Army, eventually replaced by the M-16. It fires the standard NATO 7.62 mm round.

M-16—Became the standard infantry weapon of the Vietnam War. It fires 5.56 mm ammunition.

M-79—Short-barreled, shoulder-fired weapon that fires a 40 mm grenade, which can be high-explosive, white phosphorus or canister.

MACV—Military Assistance Command, Vietnam. Replaced MAAG—the Military Assistance Advisory Group—in 1964.

MEDEVAC—Medical Evacuation. Dustoff. Helicopter used to take wounded to medical facilities.

MIA—Missing In Action.

NCO—Noncommission Officer. Noncom. Sergeant.

NCOIC—NCO In Charge. Senior NCO in a unit, detachment or a patrol.

NEXT—The man who said he was the next to be rotated home. See *Short-timer*.

NINETEEN—Average age of the combat soldier in Vietnam, in contrast to age twenty-six in the Second World War.

NOUC-MAM—Foul smelling fermented fish sauce used by the Vietnamese as a condiment.

NVA—North Vietnamese Army. Also used to designate a soldier from North Vietnam.

OD—Olive Drab, the standard military color.

P-38—Military designation for the small one-piece can opener supplied with C-rations.

PETA-PRIME—Black tarlike substance that melted in the heat of the day to become a sticky black nightmare that clung to boots, clothes and equipment. It was used to hold down the dust during the dry season.

PETER PILOT—Copilot of a helicopter.

POW—Prisoner Of War.

POGUES—Derogatory term describing fat, lazy people who inhabited rear areas, taking all the best supplies for themselves and leaving the rest for the men in the field.

PSP—Perforated Steel Plate used instead of pavement for runways and roadways.

PULL PITCH—Term used by helicopter pilots that means they are going to take off.

PUNJI STAKE—Sharpened bamboo stake hidden to penetrate the foot, sometimes dipped in feces to increase the likelihood of infection.

QT—Quick Time. It came to mean talking to someone quietly on the side rather than operating in official channels.

R AND R—Rest and Relaxation. The term came to mean a trip outside Vietnam where the soldier could forget about the war.

RF STRIKERS—Local military forces recruited and employed inside a province. Known as Regional Forces.

RINGKNOCKER—Graduate of a military academy. The term refers to the ring worn by all graduates.

RPD—7.62 mm Soviet light machine gun.

RTO—Radiotelephone operator. Radio man of a unit.

RULES OF ENGAGEMENT—Rules telling American troops when they could fire. Full Suppression meant they could fire all the way in on a landing. Normal Rules meant they could return fire for fire received. Negative Suppression meant they weren't to shoot back.

SAPPER—Enemy soldier trained in use of demolitions. Used explosives during attacks.

SHIT HOOK—Name applied by troops to the Chinook helicopter because of all the "shit" stirred up by the massive rotors.

SHORT—Term used by a GI in Vietnam to tell all who would listen that his tour was almost over.

SHORT-TIMER—GI who had been in Vietnam for nearly a year and who would be rotated back to the World soon. When the DEROS (Date of Estimated Return From Overseas Service) was the shortest in the unit, the person was said to be *Next*.

SIX—Radio call sign for the Unit Commander.

SKS—Simonov 7.62 mm semiautomatic carbine.

SMG—Submachine gun.

SOI—Signal Operating Instructions. The booklet that contained the call signs and radio frequencies of the units in Vietnam.

SOP—Standard Operating Procedure.

STEEL POT—Standard U.S. Army helmet. It consisted of a fiber helmet liner with an outer steel cover.

STORMY WEATHER—Code name for the Cambodian border.

TAI—Vietnamese ethnic group living in the mountainous regions.

TEAM UNIFORM—UHF radio frequency on which the team communicates. Frequencies were changed periodically in an attempt to confuse the enemy.

THREE—Radio call sign of the Operations Officer.

THREE CORPS—Military area around Saigon. Vietnam was divided into four corps areas.

TOC—Tactical Operations Center.

TOT—Time Over Target. Refers to the time the aircraft are supposed to be over the drop zone with the parachutists, or the target if the planes are bombers.

TWO—Radio call sign of the Intelligence Officer.

TWO-OH-ONE (201) FILE—Military records file that listed all a soldier's qualifications, training, experience and abilities. It was passed from unit to unit so that the new commander would have some idea of the incoming soldier's capabilities.

VC—Vietcong. Also Victor Charlie (phonetic alphabet) or Charlie.

VIETCONG—Contraction of Vietnam Cong San (Vietnamese Communist Party, established in 1956.)

WIA—Wounded In Action.

WILLIE PETE—WP. White Phosphorus. Smoke Rounds. Also used as antipersonnel weapons.

WORLD—United States. Always referred to as "the World."

XO—Executive Officer of a unit.

ZIPPO—A flamethrower.

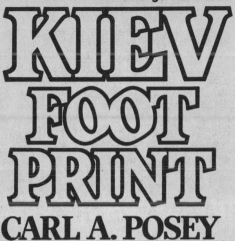

4 FREE BOOKS
1 FREE GIFT
NO RISK
NO OBLIGATION
NO KIDDING